LOVE HER? SURE . . .
BUT COULD HE TRUST HER?

Her name was Sara Colvin. She danced pagan numbers in a Texas cabaret . . . and passed heroin on the side. But she had principles. She'd waited, she told Rack Ramsey, until the right man came along . . .

Rack believed her. Only it didn't jibe — not the way she cuddled up to her boss, Blake Bowen . . . not with a murder she knew more about than she was telling.

And then came that night on the beach when at last he knew her for what she was!

"A swift, passion-filled story packed with excitement and surprise." —*Durham HERALD*

FROM THE REVIEWS

"This is a suspenseful murder story in which gamblers and other racketeers play fast and loose, and the police enter only after all is settled." —*Chattanooga TIMES*

"JUDAS JOURNEY has that rare quality, bridled realism. The author has nicely blended adventure, mystery and passion into a credible narrative . . . Perhaps the most notable feature of JUDAS JOURNEY is that it is definitely in the 'tough' category, without reading like a neurotic adolescent's daydream. Anyone who enjoys a really good detectve novel can find excellent entertainment in JUDAS JOURNEY."

—*Sioux City JOURNAL*

"A swift, passion-filled story packed with excitement and surprise." —*Durham HERALD*

"Exciting enough to please the most avid whodunit fan . . . Swift pace, colorful characters and bright dialogue make it entertaining." —*Fort Wayne SENTINEL*

A SUSPENSE NOVEL

JUDAS JOURNEY

LEE ROBERTS
AUTHOR OF "THE PALE DOOR"

WILDSIDE PRESS

Judas Journey

Published by Wildside Press LLC
www.wildsidepress.com

For Marde and Jo

CHAPTER 1

THE TAXI DRIVER said, "Along here some place?"

Ramsey peered out of the window. Ahead he saw the curving drive leading up to Marcia's place, and through the rain he could make out the dark outline of the big house on the hill. "Yes," he said, "the next drive."

The taxi turned, swung up the hill and stopped before the terrace. Rain bounced and spattered on the tile and Ramsey remembered the first afternoon when he'd sat on the terrace in the wind with Marcia. Light glowed through the French doors beyond and through the rain-streaked glass he saw a dim, slowly moving figure.

The driver said, "Want me to wait, Jack?"

"No." Ramsey paid him and got out. He stood in the rain until the taxi had circled the drive back down to the highway. Then he ran across the terrace and rapped softly on the door. It opened immediately. He stepped inside, kicked the door shut and removed his rain-spotted hat.

She looked marvelous, he thought, as she had always looked. Erect and slim, with glossy black hair falling over her shoulders. Her lips were parted and her dark eyes searched his face. She was wearing a pale blue silk robe, long and sheer and clinging, and in one hand she held a tall glass, the ice in it tinkling gently. The rain beating on the windows reminded Ramsey of another night three months before.

"Rack," she whispered, "oh, Rack . . ." With a trembling hand she placed the glass on a low table, and then stepped into his arms.

"You'll get wet," he said. "My coat is wet . . ." Her lips were on his, clinging fiercely, and he forgot the rainy night and the marvelous forest of mahogany, and he forgot the jungle and Nevil Simpson; he even forgot the sight of the fer-de-lance and its fangs clinging to Pete Davos' wrist. He forgot Sara Colvin and Phil Stark and Blake Bowen,

5

and all those people in the past, and he remembered only the last three days with Marcia, before he'd gone to Mexico.

She whispered against his lips, "I've missed you, Rack. Hold me . . ."

Abruptly the moment of forgetfulness was over, and Ramsey pushed her roughly away. She stared at him, her eyes bewildered, her mouth trembling. "I still love you, Rack. Really, I do. Let me explain . . ."

"You wrote me a letter—remember?" He unbuttoned his raincoat, took a folded paper from an inside pocket and held it up. "You said you weren't the waiting kind."

"I—I didn't mean it, Rack. I was so lonesome for you, but Jeff, he—"

"You're married to Jeff now," he broke in, trying to keep his voice steady. "Why did you ask me here tonight? What do you want of me now?"

She gazed at him with sad, brooding eyes. "I had hoped you would understand. I remember . . ." She made a small helpless gesture and turned away.

He knew what she was remembering. He was remembering, too. He saw the smooth arch of her back beneath the thin robe and the way her hair fell over her shoulders, and something inside of him seemed to coil slowly.

She stooped, took a cigarette from a silver box on the low table and turned, holding the cigarette and gazing at him expectantly. It was an old gesture; she was asking him to light her cigarette. He stepped forward, picked up a booklet of matches lying beside the silver box and struck a light. As she lowered her gaze to the flame, he glanced at the match cover. It was black and silver and embossed words jumped out at him: *The Starlight Club . . . Phil Stark, Owner . . .*

She stepped back a little and watched him with grave eyes. Smoke from her cigarette drifted upward in the silent room. He tossed the match folder to the table. "So you know Phil Stark?"

"Yes. He was here tonight. That's why I couldn't see you earlier."

"Friend of yours?"

"No. He was here on—business." She drew on the cigarette, watching him. "Do you know Phil?"

"I met him tonight. He offered me a job. Did you tell

6

him that your husband was out of town—as you told me?"

Sudden tears were in her eyes. "Rack, why do you talk like this? Phil Stark means nothing to me. He's just a—a gambler." She moved closer to him. "He came to see me about Jeff."

He was surprised. "Jeff?"

"Yes," she said bitterly, "my dear husband. It seems that he owes Phil twenty thousand dollars—a gambling debt. Phil wanted to know what I was going to do about it."

"Well," Ramsey said evenly, "you've got the money in the family."

"Yes," she said in a brittle voice, "I know very well why Jeff married me. And I told Phil that I didn't intend to do anything about the twenty thousand. I'm all finished doing things for Jeff. I'm going to divorce him, Rack. That's what I wanted to tell you."

Ramsey took a deep breath. "You promised to wait until I came back. Why did you marry him?"

"I—I didn't want to, Rack, believe me . . ." She picked up the glass and took a long swallow.

"Shotgun wedding?" he asked mockingly.

She gazed at him over the rim of the glass. "We'd been to a party. There was a lot to drink, too much." She turned partially away and drew on her cigarette. "It was just one of those things—all part of a merry evening. We chartered a plane to Mexico, a party of us, and—Jeff and I were married. A gay lark, I thought—until afterward. Then I was sorry, of course, but there wasn't much I could do about it. Jeff's a lawyer, you know, and he played it smart—maneuvered the whole thing. I know now that he had it all planned . . ." She turned to face him and her lips twisted. "I was his legal wife, and that's all Jeff wanted."

"I see," Ramsey said. "So you were stuck with Jeff and bored with him, and you began to chase around with Blake Bowen."

"Why shouldn't I? You were down in the jungles of Mexico on a silly wild goose chase for mahogany, and Jeff —well, I'd rather not discuss Jeff. And Blake was kind to me, in his way, and—you shouldn't have left me, Rack, not for so long. You know how I am."

"Yes, I know," he said. "Everything is wonderful. While I'm gone you marry a cold-blooded lawyer, and have an affair with a cheap night club owner, and God knows what

7

else. What am I supposed to do? Kiss and make up to a married woman?"

"Listen, Rack—I'm going to divorce Jeff, no matter what it costs me. I want you to know that."

"And marry me?"

"If you still want me."

"Jeff will fight the divorce."

"Of course, but I'll win. . . . Do you still love me, Rack.'"

"Yes," he said, thinking that in spite of everything he really meant it.

Her eyes became tender and the soft light made shadows on her cheeks and glinted with a moist redness on her full lips. She was beautiful, he thought, very desirable, even though she had lived fast, according to her whims of the moment, with never a thought of the morning or of what lurked beyond the next hour. That was the way she was made, and it was money that had ruined her, the money her father had left her. It had made her what she was, and maybe he could even understand why she had married Jefferson Carr. It was the kind of thing she would do—and then regret in the cold bleak dawn. And he knew that he still wanted her, in spite of everything. It would be stupid of him not to want her—and her millions.

"I need you, Rack," she whispered. "You need me." She placed her glass on the table, crushed out her cigarette. Then she stood erect, her hands at her side, the palms turned outward in invitation, and there was a melting softness in her eyes and around her lips, an almost virginal shyness. Her body moved beneath the robe and she gave him a small tremulous smile.

It was a smile that Ramsey would never forget.

As he moved toward her, the room rocked with a blinding explosion. For a vivid instant the windows gleamed red with a flash of fire. Marcia Carr's head jerked backward, like a puppet on a string, and a small black hole appeared beneath her right eye. She stood rigidly, a final bright gleam of life in her eyes, and then her face crumpled, and her body too, and her eyes went dull and dead. She fell backward to the floor, her limp body making a soft thudding sound on the thick rug.

Ramsey stared stupidly, his voice trapped in his throat. The shock of what he saw was too great; his mind refused to accept it. He heard a furtive scurrying sound behind him and as he turned slowly and dumbly a hard object slammed viciously against the side of his head, jarring him to his heels. He swayed gently, wild lights dancing in his brain, and his eyes suddenly refused to focus. His knees went limp and the floor slanted upward and through a final shimmering haze he saw the body of Marcia on the floor, the sheer folds of the blue robe spread like a silken fan beneath her.

In an odd blurred way, before the complete blackness closed in, his brain turned slowly backward, back to October . . .

' CHAPTER 2

IN OCTOBER Ramsey and Pete Davos quit their jobs in a Pennsylvania coal mine and drifted west to the oil fields of the Texas gulf coast. Ramsey went to work as a rigger and Pete landed a job as a driller's helper. They took a room at the Gulf Hotel, a small clean establishment close to the waterfront, and started work on a Monday morning. Monday evening they were drinking beer in a small night club not far from the hotel. It was called the Jungle Tavern. The decorations consisted of fake palm trees, bamboo furniture and south sea murals. The waiters wore white mess jackets and the cigarette girls swished about in brief grass skirts and little else.

It was in the Jungle Tavern that Ramsey met Sara Colvin.

She glided out onto the floor under a blue spotlight and began to sway to the savage beat of drums. Her long black hair hung over her naked shoulders and her costume consisted of a feathered headdress and a scanty two-piece arrangement of bright beads. For ten minutes her small white body writhed slowly in a dance that had been old at the time of the Aztecs. When it was over, she ran lightly from the floor. The lights came on and the six-piece orchestra began to play a rumba. The small dance floor filled with couples.

Thinking of the dancer, Ramsey said, "That's for me." He was a big man, with blond hair cropped short and a jutting ledge of brow over deep-set gray eyes. His face was still pale from the coal mine and his nose was slightly crooked, the result of a bar room brawl in Akron, Ohio. Beneath a gray tweed jacket his shoulders were thick and wide.

Pete Davos grinned across the table at him. "See if she's got a girl friend, Rack." Light glinted on Pete's heavy dark features and short curly black hair. The two men had met in the army, and after their discharge they had stuck together, drifting, following the sun, working on construction jobs, in steel mills and coal mines, in factories, wherever they could find work where they happened to be. Ramsey had been a derrick rigger before his enlistment, and this had prompted their trip to Texas. Perhaps in a month they would be in California or Florida. It didn't matter to them. They were rootless, with no particular ambitions and no interest in political, moral or civic matters. Both were single, with no family ties, except Pete Davos, who had a married sister in Saginaw. Ramsey was thirty-two years old: Pete was two years younger.

Ramsey beckoned to a hovering waiter. "What's her name? The dancer?"

"Sara Colvin, sir."

"Miss Colvin?"

"I believe so, sir."

"Miss or Missus," Pete muttered. "Since when did you care?"

Ramsey ignored him, borrowed a pencil from the waiter and wrote on a corner of a menu: *I enjoyed your dance. May I buy you a drink? Please? Rackwell Ramsey*. He grinned up at the waiter, handed him the menu and a dollar. "Will you please give this to her—and bring us two more beers?"

The waiter nodded, his face impassive, and moved away.

Pete said eagerly, "Did you mention a girl for me?"

"I will," Ramsey said. "Everything in proper order."

One hour and three beers later it was midnight. Sara Colvin danced again, this time in an off-shoulder peasant

10

blouse and a swirling red skirt. Once she looked directly at Ramsey. He grinned and lifted a hand. She glanced quickly away and did not look toward him again. Her hair was now coiled in two thick braids around her small delicately shaped head. Ramsey saw that her eyes were brown and tilted slightly at the outer corners. Part Mex, he thought, or maybe Chinese, and a slow excitement stirred within him.

When the dance was over, she smiled, half shyly, blew a kiss at the crowd, and was gone with a flash of slim white legs beneath the red skirt.

Ramsey finished his beer, put some money on the table and stood up. "Come on," he said to Pete. Out on the sidewalk Ramsey hesitated and then said to Pete. "I'll go around in back. You wait here—so we don't miss her."

"All right," Pete said, "but I'm sleepy—and don't forget we gotta be on the job at seven."

"Sure," Ramsey said. "It's only a little after one. Don't you want me to ask her if she's got a girl friend?"

Pete said sullenly, "You ain't interested in no girl friend."

"Why, sure I am, Pete, boy. I'll ask her the first thing."

"I'll bet," Pete sneered. "I can see you got my interests at heart. I'll stay here for ten minutes. If she don't show by then, I'm hitting the sack."

Ramsey grinned at him, lit a cigarette and walked through a dark alley to a small court at the rear of the Jungle Tavern. There were cement steps and a small stoop, with a light burning over a door. There was no signs, but Ramsey was familiar with such things, and he was certain that Sara Colvin would leave by this door. He leaned against the wall in shadow and drew on his cigarette. A light fog was coming in off the gulf and the air was soft and cool. Presently the door opened. The dancer came out and stood for a moment under the dim light. Then she went down the steps and walked swiftly across the court toward the street, her heels making swift clicking sounds on the cement. She was wearing a simple black dress, but no hat, and she carried a light coat and a small purse.

Ramsey snapped his cigarette away and stepped out of the shadow. "Miss Colvin," he called softly.

She paused, turned her head, and waited uncertainly as he moved up to her. She was smaller than he had thought;

11

the top of her head was a full six inches below his chin. He smiled down at her. "You got my note?"

"I get many notes," she said coolly, with just the faintest whisper of an accent.

"Ramsey is the name," he said easily. "Maybe you remember?"

A faint smile touched her lips. "Rackwell," she said. "I remember it because it is such an odd name." The smile went away and she asked gravely, "What do you want?"

"The note said I'd like to buy you a drink."

"No, thank you."

He smiled and nodded. "All right. But you won't mind if I tell you that I admired your dancing?"

"I do not object to that," she said in the same grave voice. "Thank you."

"May I take you home?"

She shook her head, gazing up at him soberly.

"Why not?" It was an old game with him. Her nearness excited him, and he warned himself to go slow. He knew already that she was not just another night club dancer, not just another pick-up. The quality of her voice, the faint accent and her quiet bearing told him that. She was something a little special, he thought; in fact, her cool poise disturbed him. It was not going to be as easy as he had anticipated. "Please," he said.

"I am afraid not," she said shortly. "Good night." She turned and moved away.

He caught her arm, not roughly; he was careful about it. There was a time for roughness, and a time for gentleness. "Please," he said again. "I am very lonely tonight. I liked your dancing and I thought it would be nice to meet you, to talk with you a little . . . " He dropped his hand from her arm and stood smiling.

She gazed up at him, her eyes troubled. "Loneliness—it is a bad thing."

He nodded, watching her.

"You have no family, no—wife?"

He shook his head. "No wife. Not anybody for a long time. My parents died when I was in the army—both of them, in a train wreck, while they were coming to see me in camp, before I shipped out."

As he spoke, he thought suddenly and with sadness that this was true. It seemed a long time ago. They had given

12

him a special pass to go home to the funeral, and he remembered the chill rain in the cemetery and the mud from the new double grave which had clung to his polished dress oxfords, the embarrassed expressions of sympathy from old family friends and a few distant relatives—all scattered to hell and gone now, with nobody remembering or caring about Rackwell Ramsey, the only son of Maude and Gilbert Ramsey who had been killed in that train wreck that time so long ago. He thought of his father, a big quiet man who for the most part of his adult life had been a meter reader for the power company in Toledo, Ohio, and of his mother, plump and pretty.

"I am sorry." Sara Colvin's voice seemed to come to him from out of the past.

Ramsey peered at her in the gloom and smiled. He hadn't meant to arouse her sympathy in the way he had, but he was pleased with his luck. He touched her arm. "Where shall we go?"

"I—I would like some coffee. There is a little place around the corner . . .' '

"Coffee?" he scoffed.

"Yes," she said firmly.

"Sure. Whatever you want." He guided her around the corner to the entrance of the Jungle Tavern. Pete Davos was standing there looking sleepy and bored.

As they approached, Sara Colvin said, "Is not that your friend? The one who was with you inside?"

"Yes." Ramsey stopped in front of Pete. "Miss Colvin, this is my friend Pete Davos."

She held out her hand and smiled.

Pete took her hand, moved his feet awkwardly, and gave Ramsey a dark look.

Ramsey said politely, "Pete, would you care to join us in a cup of coffee?"

"Naw—I'm going back to the hotel." He moved away.

"Goodbye, Pete," the girl said.

"Goodbye," Pete mumbled. "Glad to have met you." He disappeared around the corner.

As Ramsey and the girl walked along the sidewalk, she said. "He seems nice."

"He's my buddy. We've been together a long time."

They entered a small restaurant and found a booth in a corner. The hot black coffee tasted good to Ramsey after the beer. In the bright light he saw that the girl was younger than he'd first guessed. Her skin held a soft smooth quality and her brown eyes were bright and clear. At first she seemed shy and kept watching him in an odd way. He touched her hand and smiled. "Don't be afraid. I'm just an ordinary guy.

"I'm not afraid," she said seriously. "It's just that it seems strange, being with you like this. I do not go out very much."

"We'll fix that. What're you doing tomorrow night?"

She smiled. Her teeth were small and even and very white. "You do not know yet if you like me."

"I liked you the minute I saw you." He began to talk to her, and gradually he saw that the shyness was leaving her. Twice she laughed at his accounts of amusing incidents involving him and Pete. They ordered more coffee and eventually he learned that she had been born in Mexico City, that her father had been an American mining engineer, her mother Mexican. When she was ten years old her mother had run away with a bull fighter from Taxco, and her father, after a time, had quietly hung himself from a cottonwood tree.

She told it calmly. "It seems long ago. I do not feel anything any more, except that my father, he—he was nice."

"Yes," Ramsey said, thinking of his own father.

After her father's death, she told him, an aunt, a sister of her mother, had taken her to live in Mazatlan with her uncle and seven little Mexican cousins. The aunt had taught her to dance. When she was eighteen, her father's insurance money was gone and she had decided to come to the States. Through a New York agency she had found work right away and for the past three years had been dancing in night clubs and hotels in various parts of the country. Once she'd had a chorus spot in a musical that folded in Boston, and had made several minor television appearances. She had been at the Jungle Tavern for over a month, and hoped to eventually work her way to California and maybe get some movie jobs.

"I am not a very good dancer," she said, "but it is all I know how to do."

"You're a wonderful dancer," he said, and added, "What about your love life?" It was time the subject was

14

mentioned, he thought. "Any boy friends? I mean, anyone special?"

She shook her head quickly. "I have met many men, but I have not stayed in one place long enough to really get acquainted with them."

"Good," he said, smiling, and touching her hand. She didn't draw her hand away. He suggested leaving then, and she agreed.

The fog was thicker and the street lights glowed yellowly through it, making a glistening dampness on the pavement. A taxi rolled along the curb toward them. Ramsey took the girl's arm and started for it.

"No," she said. "Let us walk. I live only a few blocks from here."

Ramsey waved the taxi on. Ten minutes later they came to a small neat brick apartment building on a quiet side street. There was a clipped hedge and a small tiled stoop flanked by a wrought-iron railing. Ramsey followed the girl into a small dimly-lighted foyer containing a single telephone booth, a row of mail boxes, a door labeled *Office* and an automatic elevator. She turned to face him.

"It has been nice," she said. "Thank you very much for bringing me home."

He was surprised. "Aren't you going to ask me up?"

She gazed at him gravely. "Did you expect me to?"

"I had hoped you would."

"Why?"

He was a little disconcerted, but he said easily, "Maybe have a nightcap, talk—the usual reasons."

Her eyes hardened a little. "I'm afraid you have been wasting your time."

He moved close, placed an arm around her small waist and tilted her chin with a finger. "Please," he said softly.

She stood stiffly within his arm. "Let me go," she said in a low voice.

He forced her against him and kissed her. She didn't resist, but her lips were cold. The time for gentleness is past, he thought, and he looked beyond her at the mail boxes on the wall. A white card on one of them read: *Sara Colvin—3-D*. He pushed her into the elevator and pressed a button numbered *3*. As the door closed and they began to move upward, he looked down at her. There were tears on her cheeks and her eyes were tightly closed. He was sur-

15

prised and a little shocked. He let her go, aware that the elevator had stopped and that the door had slid open. Blindly she moved past him into a green-carpeted hall. He started to follow her. "Listen," he said. "I'm sorry. I—"

She turned a corner of the hall and disappeared. He stood still. There was the sound of a key turning in a lock, and a door opened and closed firmly with a final click. He stood in the silence, bewildered. Hell, he'd picked her up, a part Mex gal who danced almost naked in a sucker trap —what did she expect?

He hesitated a moment, then decided against knocking on her door. She had made it clear that she did not want him. He sighed, shook his head and entered the elevator.

CHAPTER 3

PETE DAVOS was waiting for him in the lobby of the Gulf Hotel. "How was it?" Pete asked, grinning.

"Shut up." Ramsey strode past him.

"Aw, Rack," Pete protested, hurrying after him. "I was just asking. I been waiting for you, Rack." He grasped Ramsey's arm.

Ramsey stopped and turned. "I thought you were going to bed."

"I was, but there's somebody I met in the bar. I want you to meet him."

"I'm tired. Who is it?"

"You'll see," Pete said, grinning. "Come on." He pulled the reluctant Ramsey across the lobby.

They entered a long murky room with a bar against one wall, booths along the other, tables in the center. Pete led Ramsey to a table at the far end. As they approached, a man stood up and gazed at them steadily, swaying a little. He was a very thin man with wide spare shoulders. His narrow face and the top of his bald head were burned dark by the sun, and the yellow hair over his ears was bleached almost white. His nose was long, with sensitive nostrils; his mouth and chin were firm. He wore a rather scraggly

16

yellow mustache and his eyes behind gold-rimmed glasses were the pale blue of a winter sky. A dark blue serge suit hung limply on his lean frame and a black knit tie was knotted loosely in the collar of a soft white shirt. He was about fifty years old.

"My God," Ramsey said, grinning broadly. "Simpson." He held out a hand. The thin man reached for it, missed, and Ramsey grabbed his.

"Rackwell," Simpson said gravely, "it is nice to see you again." He pointed a long wavering finger at Pete Davos. "When I saw Pete come in, I couldn't believe my eyes." He peered down over his glasses at the table. "I see that I have received a fresh drink. Will you join me?"

The three of them sat down. Simpson motioned to a waiter, gave their order, and then said to Ramsey, "I am quite drunk, Rackwell. I hope you will forgive me."

"Don't mention it. Are you out here on a job?"

"I was," Simpson said, "but it is finished. Down Tampico way—for an American mining company. Consulting job." He smiled at the two men. "As they say in the theatrical world, I am currently at liberty." He drank from a tall glass which Ramsey knew contained Scotch and water, knowing Simpson's drinking habits as he did.

Nevil Simpson was a geologist, a free-lancer, who worked mostly as a consultant. Ramsey and Pete had met him in Pennsylvania when he'd been doing some special strata testing for the coal mine. The two men had been assigned to help Simpson, and in the six weeks it had taken to complete the tests the three of them had become good friends. When Simpson left, they had promised to write each other, but they never had. Ramsey was genuinely pleased to see the grave and friendly geologist.

Pete touched Simpson's arm. "Tell him about it," he said eagerly.

Ramsey grinned at Simpson. "Don't tell me you got married again?"

Simpson sighed and fixed Ramsey with bright and somewhat glazed eyes. "No, Rackwell," he said sadly, "my marital situation remains unchanged. I wish it were otherwise, but my beloved ex-wife still refuses to share my roving life." He sighed again. "Pete is referring to the mahogany."

Ramsey looked puzzled. "Mahogany?"

Simpson nodded solemnly. "A veritable forest, a virgin stand. Fabulous." He drank from his glass.

Ramsey gave Pete a questioning glance. "Go on," Pete said to Simpson. "Tell him."

Simpson leaned forward and peered at Ramsey. His blue eyes seemed to swirl in his head. "Pure luck," he said gravely, "meeting you and Pete like this. Would you be interested in going after the mahogany?"

"I don't know." Ramsey winked at Pete. "Where is it?"

Simpson took an envelope from an inside coat pocket, laid it on the table, produced the yellow stub of a pencil and drew a wavering line. "That, gentlemen, is the Rio Verde in the Mexican state of San Luis Potosi." An inch from the line he made a cross. "And there is the mahogany." He drained his glass in one long swallow and said softly, "Virgin, Rackwell. Fabulous." His gaze shifted and focused waveringly on a spot above Ramsey's head. "Excuse me," he mumbled. He closed his eyes and his head sank slowly to the table.

Ramsey looked at Pete, shook his head slowly and stood up.

Pete grasped Ramsey's arm. "Listen, Rack, he's on the level. We just met in the bar and got to talking, and then he began to tell men about the mahogany. He was a little drunk, but not like he is now, and the more he talked the more I believed him. It's like he said; he was down there in Mexico working for the mining company, making some kind of survey, and he found the mahogany, a forest of it, way the hell back in the bush. Rack, he wants us to throw in with him—form a—an expedition, he said. We'll all be rich."

Ramsey laughed. "Oh, sure."

"No, Rack, listen," Pete said excitedly. "It makes sense. When he found the mahogany he was with a crew of ignorant working stiffs, Mexicans, dumb as hell. They didn't pay no attention to the mahogany, and Simpson didn't tell anybody about it—just us. He was trying to find somebody he could trust to go in with him, and we show up. He made a map of the location and he wants to go back, to see if there's a way to get the wood out to the coast, but he don't have enough money, and besides it's a job for at least three men—the supplies to carry, and all. There's a road part way, but it peters out and we'll have to walk in. There ain't

18

no roads back there, Simpson said, and no places for a plane to land, just swamp and hills and jungle. But it's there, Rack, all that mahogany. Think of it—the money!"

A little of Pete's excitement was communicated to Ramsey. He had respect for Simpson's education and intelligence, and he gazed thoughtfully at the sleeping geologist. "We'll talk to him when he's sober," he told Pete. "But we can't leave him here."

"He's got a room upstairs," Pete said. "He told me he'd been here a week."

Ramsey reached into Simpson's coat pocket, found a tabbed key and said to Pete, "Two-o-six." He paid the check and a sympathetic waiter told them they could take their friend up a back stairway. They got Simpson out of the bar, ignoring the amused glances of the other patrons, and up the stairs. Pete supported Simpson while Ramsey unlocked the door of room 206. As they laid Simpson on the bed, his wallet fell from his coat pocket. It lay open on the floor and when Ramsey picked it up he saw the contents of two cellophaned sections. A card in one certified that Nevil H. Simpson, of St. Louis, Missouri, was a member in good standing of the Geological Society of America. The other compartment held a faded snapshot of a pretty dark-haired woman in a white dress standing in bright sunlight beside a palm tree with the white roofs of a tropical village on the far hills behind her.

Pete peered over Ramsey's shoulder. "Must be his wife."

"Ex-wife," Ramsey said. "Pretty, huh? Must have been taken in the days before she divorced him, before she decided she wanted to settle down in one place." He sighed and replaced the wallet in the coat pocket. They undressed Simpson to his underwear and covered him up. As they left, they heard him mumble, "Fabulous . . . Virgin . . ."

The clerk called them at six o'clock, as they had instructed. Sleepily and mechanically they dressed in their working clothes of blue jeans, flannel shirts and heavy shoes. Years of conditioning had hardened them to getting up and going to work after a few hours sleep, or no sleep at all, often with wicked hangovers. It was part of the life they led, and they accepted it without complaint. Ramsey had long ago learned that there was a price for everything and that it was merely a matter of choice and how much you

19

paid, in one way or another, for pleasures of goods received. This morning he was tired, but his head was clear, and he was faintly annoyed to realize that he was thinking of the little dancer at the Jungle Tavern. What was her name? Sara something.

Pete yawned, picked up his leather jacket and metal lunch box. "Well, come on. If we wanna eat, we gotta work."

They left the room they shared and as they passed Simpson's door, Pete paused and listened a moment. "Not a peep," he said, grinning. "He's still dead to the world."

Ramsey merely grunted. It was funny, he thought, still thinking of the dancer. She had let him pick her up, and then pulled the innocent, hard-to-get act.

In the restaurant down stairs they ate ham and eggs, fried potatoes, brown bread toast and drank hot coffee from thick mugs. The Gulf Hotel catered to oil field workers, and the cook filled their lunch boxes with sandwiches, pie and coffee. Then they went out into the fresh morning and caught a bus to the field.

It was almost six o'clock when they returned to the hotel, tired and muddy. After a bath and a change of clothes they went down to the bar. Simpson was sitting at a table with a full glass before him. He stood up as they entered and smiled a little ruefully. He was wearing the same blue suit, but his shirt was fresh and white, his yellow mustache was neatly trimmed, and his blue eyes behind the gold-rimmed glasses were bright and clear.

Pete waved, grinning, "Hi, Simpson."

Ramsey thought with affection that if Pete had been a dog his tail would be wagging. Life was simple for Pete, and he didn't ask or expect much. He was friendly and easy-going, but fiercely loyal to Ramsey. On a number of occasions Pete's hard fists had helped to get them out of unfriendly and even dangerous situations in which they sometimes found themselves, usually in a bar.

"Good evening," Simpson said in his grave voice. "I have been waiting for you, to apologize for my disgraceful conduct last night, and to thank you for putting me to bed, where I most certainly belonged. I am afraid that I sometimes misjudge my capacity for alcohol, especially after a dry time in the field. Who paid the check last night?"

"I did," Ramsey said, "but forget it."

"Thank you, Rackwell. I wish to reimburse you."

Ramsey said, "You bought us plenty of drinks in Pittsburgh."

"Then I insist upon buying now. Will you join me?"

They ordered drinks—another Scotch and water for Simpson, Bourbon and soda for Ramsey and Pete. As Ramsey relaxed in the chair he became aware of the tiredness of his muscles and he told himself that right after dinner he would go to bed. Then he thought of the dancer, Sara— what was her last name? Colvin, that was it—and he stirred restlessly.

Simpson said, "Have you two thought over what I told you last night?"

Ramsey smiled. "I'm afraid not. After all, you didn't give us a very clear picture."

Simpson smiled wryly. "Again I apologize. But what I told you is true. It seemed natural to tell you and Pete. I'm all alone now; my friends are scattered around the globe. My wife, as you know, divorced me and I can't say that I blame her. A woman wants roots and security." He paused and sipped moodily at his drink. "I presume I have told you about Angeline?"

"Yes," Ramsey said, remembering the days in Pittsburgh.

Simpson sighed. "Angeline wanted a permanent home, and children—all the trite and maybe wonderful things that every woman wants. I don't blame her. But geology is my work, my life, and I had to go where the work was. Oh, I could have taken a professorship at some university, and Angeline would have loved being a faculty wife, but I guess I'm just a rover at heart, like you, Rackwell, and you, Pete. The far horizon, you know, the view from the next mountain-top, the turn in the road and all that foolish and romantic nonsense." He drank again. "Maybe I'm sorry, now that I'm getting along in years. I still write to Angeline, and she writes to me. She's teaching natural history in a high school in St. Louis, and living with her parents." He reached inside his coat. "I have a photo of Angeline, taken years ago in Brazil. . . ."

"What about the mahogany?" Ramsey asked gently.

"Ah, yes." Simpson's hand came away from the coat pocket and he wiped his glasses on a paper napkin. "It's there, Rackwell, truly. A virgin stand. Acres of mahogany

21

trees, sixty to eighty feet tall, in a remote and desolate country. I staked it out and made a preliminary survey. There will be complications—with the Mexican government, for one—but they can be worked out. The important thing now is to make a complete survey and plan a method of transportation to the coast. We will need financial help, but that can come later. It won't be easy, but if we succeed I would not attempt to estimate our gain. . . ."

Simpson paused, hooked the glasses over his ears, and continued in a soft voice. "Maybe Angeline would take me back then, if I would settle down and live the kind of life she wants. With the mahogany money, we could do that." He smiled at Ramsey and Pete. "You see? This means much more to me than mere financial gain."

"I see," Ramsey said. He had never thought of mahogany before, except as a wood from which the costlier furniture was made, but listening to Nevil Simpson's precise voice had given it an illusive glamor. "How much would it cost?"

Simpson shrugged. "I estimate that the preliminary expedition would require about three thousand dollars, and three to four months' time." He peered at Ramsey and Pete. "A thousand dollars for each of us."

"We can scrape that up," Ramsey said, thinking that it would wipe out the savings accounts he and Pete had in a Pittsburgh bank. He looked at Pete. "What do you say?"

"Let's go," Pete breathed, his dark eyes shining.

Simpson said, "I cannot promise you anything, except that the mahogany is there."

"We understand," Ramsey said. He and Pete had nothing much to lose, he thought, except their savings and a few months' time. But money could always be earned again, and time meant nothing to them. He lifted his glass in a silent toast. Simpson and Pete joined him.

"Then it's agreed," Simpson said. "We'll place the project on a business-like basis. I propose that we organize a legal partnership, pool our resources, purchase the necessary supplies and equipment and cross the Border. I have maps which I will show you. Time is important. Others may discover the mahogany, and the rainy season is just ending there. It will begin again in May or June, but we should be back long before then. I have a car which will take us to the jumping-off place. Then it will be a hard journey on foot through wild and treacherous country, but

22

at the end will be the—the rainbow." He smiled half shyly and his glasses glinted in the light.

"How soon can we leave?" Pete asked eagerly.

"We'll see." Simpson pursed his lips, got paper and the stub of pencil. "It will take a little time to get ready." He began to write. "We'll need food, medical supplies, guns, ammunition, machetes, netting, surveying instruments . . ."

Two hours later, after they'd eaten dinner, Ramsey left Simpson and Pete in Simpson's room poring over maps and talking about supplies. He changed his mind about going to bed and went instead to the Jungle Tavern, where he sat alone in a corner and watched Sara Colvin dance. At one o'clock, after her last dance, he walked to her apartment building and stood in the shadow of the hedge. He smoked and wondered irritably what he was doing there. At one-thirty a black Jaguar pulled up to the curb and stopped. A man and a woman got out, and Ramsey saw that the woman was Sara Colvin. The man was tall and hatless and wore a loose topcoat over a tuxedo. They walked to the door and stood talking in low tones. Then Ramsey heard her say, "Good night, Blake. Thank you."

The man said something, went back to the Jaguar and drove away. Ramsey moved quickly up behind the girl as she entered the foyer. She heard his step and turned. He saw the startled recognition in her eyes, and he felt suddenly awkward and ill at ease. "Hello," he said.

"Hello." Her voice and her eyes were cool.

"I'm sorry—about last night."

Her eyes softened. "Thank you," she said quietly. "It was nice of you to wait here to tell me—Rackwell. Is not that your name?"

"Yes, but call me Rack."

"I have thought about you today," she said, "and I have decided that perhaps you were not to blame. We were strangers to each other and I permitted you to walk home with me, and naturally you . . ." She lowered her gaze and fingered a button of her coat. He could not see the faintly mischievous gleam in her eyes.

"Naturally," he said, and he thought dismally that she really shouldn't blame him. It had been her mistake, too. What kind of a woman did she think he was looking for,

23

a man like him? He turned away and said shortly, "I won't bother you any more."

Behind him she laughed softly, a pleasant sound. "Now you are being—noble, but I accept your apology."

He paused and turned.

"Would you like to come up for a nightcap?" she asked. "The one you did not get last night?"

He felt that she was mocking him and he said stiffly, "No, thanks."

She smiled. "Of course you do, and you're welcome—now. Please come in." She turned and entered the building.

Dumbly he followed her and stood silently as the elevator took them up. As she unlocked her apartment door, he said, "Who was the man who brought you home?"

"Just my employer," she said over her shoulder. "Blake Bowen. He owns the Jungle Tavern." She opened the door and he followed her inside.

Her apartment was small, but very neat and attractively furnished. She made Bourbon highballs and talked to him about his work, about Mexico, and he relaxed and suddenly realized that he was enjoying himself. She played some Mexican records and told him more about her life south of the Border. It was after two o'clock in the morning when he stood up, thinking of the job starting at seven. "Thanks," he said, as he opened the door.

She said gently, "I have enjoyed it." She paused, her lips parted a little. "Would—would you like to kiss me good night?"

He gave her a crooked smile. "Is it safe? You won't get angry?"

She shook her small head. "One does not get angry because of a kiss given in—in friendship."

He lowered his head, not touching her with his hands. Her lips were warm and soft, and for an instant he thought of her near-nakedness in the blue spotlight as she danced. She drew away and smiled. "Good night—Rack."

"Can I see you again?"

"If you like."

"I like," he said. "I guess we kind of got off on the wrong foot last night."

"It is forgotten," she said gravely.

"Tomorrow night?"

"All right," she said, "but you go to work so early in the morning, and you need your sleep."

"Hell," he said, "I can rig a well with my eyes shut." He snapped his fingers. "Who cares about sleep?"

"Why not an early meeting?" she asked. "For dinner? I do not report for work until nearly nine o'clock."

"Fine. I'll pick you up around six. Here?"

"I will be ready."

He wanted to kiss her again. He was fairly certain that he could, but he did not want to press his luck. He stepped back and she softly closed the door. He heard the lock click, and he smiled a little grimly. It takes all kinds, he thought, as he went down the hall. He knew quite a bit about women and their tactics, but this was something a little different.

He whistled softly as he walked to the Gulf Hotel.

CHAPTER 4

THE NEXT EVENING, on a sudden impulse he could not explain, Ramsey took Sara Colvin to the Gulf Hotel for dinner with Pete and Nevil Simpson. Being previously warned by Ramsey, neither man made any mention of the planned expedition into Mexico. They both were very polite to Sara, and Ramsey saw that her quiet friendly manner pleased them. He had an odd new feeling of pride in her.

Afterward, at the rear entrance to the Jungle Tavern, she said, "I enjoyed meeting your friends, Rack."

"I could see they liked you."

"I am glad," she said soberly. "I want your friends to like me."

"What about me?"

"I want you to like me, too." She lowered her gaze. "But I know you do—otherwise you would not have wanted me to dine with your friends."

"I'll wait for you tonight," he said.

"It will be late, and you must get your sleep. . . ."

It sounded strange to him. Nobody had ever cared if

he got enough sleep, not since his mother died. He gazed at Sara Colvin and remembered his pride in her as she had talked to Pete and Simpson. "I'll get some sleep now, and meet you at one," he said.

She reached up and kissed him lightly, and then slipped through the door and was gone.

Pete was waiting for him in the room at the hotel. They wrote letters to the bank in Pittsburgh withdrawing their savings accounts. Nevil Simpson came in, and when they showed him the letters he shook hands with them gravely.

"Partners," he said in his quiet voice. "Share and share alike. I propose that Rackwell be treasurer of the operation. He is to hold all the money and pay the bills."

Ramsey protested, but Pete and Simpson were firm. "We will leave next week if possible," Simpson said. "You both had better give your foreman notice."

"I never quit a job yet without notice," Ramsey said, "but will it be that soon? Next week?"

Pete laughed. "I know what's worrying him."

Simpson smiled. "I do not blame you, Rackwell, for not wanting to leave a lovely girl like Miss Colvin. I meant to tell you that I was very favorably impressed with her— a gentle and charming personality."

"Too charming for him," Pete said. He grinned at Ramsey. "Maybe I ought to tip her off about old Rackwell, the lady's man, the great lover who meets 'em and loves 'em, and leaves 'em where he loves 'em."

"To hell with you," Ramsey said, trying not to show the odd feeling of anger he felt at Pete's friendly jibe.

"Cheer up, Rockwell," Simpson said. "Perhaps she will still be here when we return."

"And all of us loaded with dough," Pete said. "You can buy her Caddies and mink coats."

"Sure, sure," Ramsey said carelessly.

Pete and Simpson began a game of double solitaire. Ramsey took off his coat and stretched out on the bed. After a while he slept, and when he awoke the room was dark. Someone—probably Pete—had thrown a blanket over him. He went into the bathroom, turned on the light, and looked at his wrist watch. Almost one o'clock. He would have to hurry, he thought, as he washed his face, brushed his teeth and ran a comb through his short yellow hair. As he left, he heard Pete snoring softly.

She was waiting for him in the little court behind the Jungle Tavern. "Sara," he said breathlessly, "I slept longer than—"

She placed a small finger on his lips. "I knew you would be here."

"You did?" he asked, surprised.

"Of course." She smiled up at him. "Did not anyone ever believe in you, or care what happened to you?"

He took her arm and they left the court and walked along the sidewalk toward her apartment. "I guess nobody ever had a chance," he said. "I've moved around too much."

"Do you not become weary of always going from one place to another?" she asked in her faint soft accent. "Do you ever wish you could stay in one place and know your neighbors and become part of a—a community?"

"I never thought about it," he said truthfully.

"I think about it very much," she said. "I keep remembering the friendliness and the security of my aunt's home in Mazatlan." She looked up at him. "Are you going to be here long? In this city?"

"It depends upon my job," he said carefully. "The foreman said today that the company is opening some wells in Oklahoma. They may send me there."

"Will you go?"

"I don't know."

She sighed. "It is your work. My work is dancing. But I do not like to be always living in hotels and rooms and apartments. Perhaps, if I could find steady work in California, I could have a little house and a garden. I think it would be nice."

"I worked in San Diego a few years back," he said.

"Did you, Rack?" She hugged his arm. "Tell me about it."

As they walked along he told her what he knew about the state of California, and as he talked he felt a kind of tenderness for her, a new feeling for him.

When they reached her apartment they had coffee instead of whisky, and she made thin sandwiches of ham and cheese and sharp mustard. She played more records and they talked and laughed softly together. When he left at two-thirty, they made a date for the next night. At the door he kissed her, and her lips were warm and clinging.

27

He pulled her against him roughly. She murmured, "Please," and gently pushed him away. He let her go and stood gazing down at her.

She lowered her eyes and whispered, "That is the way I am."

"Sure," he said in an unsteady voice. "It's all right." And he left, quickly.

The next night, the fourth night, he said to her, "Don't the men bother you? I mean, the ones who watch you dance? Don't they ask to take you out?"

"Yes, but Blake—Mr. Bowen—he does not permit them to talk to me. He is very strict."

"He doesn't own you." There was an edge to Ramsey's voice. "He hasn't tried to stop you from seeing me."

"No," she said with a slow smile. "He does not know about you."

He had a tiny ugly thought. "You said Bowen is your boss. What else is he?"

"Nothing, Rack." She stopped smiling. "It is just that he has been—kind to me. And he does not like me to—to mix with the patrons."

"What do you mean—he's been 'kind' to you?"

"Someday, perhaps, I will tell you." She came slowly against him and pressed a cheek against his chest. "Please do not ask me now."

He was about to speak angrily, but he checked himself. What did he care? If she was sleeping with Blake Bowen, what of it? He hadn't made much progress with her, and he wondered why he bothered. All he'd had were some drinks, some food, and a lot of Mexican music, a couple of kisses and some conversation about her childhood in Mexico. And he was pulling out with Pete and Simpson in a few days . . .

"Listen," he said, "can't you wear more clothes? When you dance?"

She looked up at him quickly. "You do not care, do you?"

"I don't like it. All those dumb yokels staring at you, drooling—"

"But it does not mean anything," she broke in. "It is part of the profession, like a—a uniform. At first, I was embarrassed, but now I do not think about it." She smiled

28

shyly. "But I think I am pleased that you do not approve."

He kissed her then, and the odd tender feeling came over him again and he couldn't understand it. He left her abruptly. At the corner of the hall he glanced back. She was still standing by the door, watching him. He gave her a stiff smile and hurried to the elevator.

All of the next day in the oil field, under the towering derricks, he thought of her as he worked in the mud and the drizzling rain. Once Pete Davos said, "Hey, Rack, I got us a couple of babes lined up for Saturday night, real nice. You wanna cut loose with me, or are you all dated up with your true love?"

"Count me out," Ramsey said shortly. As he moved away, he added, "Maybe Simpson would be interested."

"Simpson's carrying a torch for his ex-wife, you know that. Listen, Rack—"

But Ramsey was too far away to hear, and he didn't look back to see Pete's puzzled frown.

The next night it was still raining. They took a taxi from the Jungle Tavern to her apartment. Ramsey was restless and irritable, a feeling which had grown during the day. He kept thinking that the next day was Saturday, and he was sorry now that he'd turned down Pete's invitation. Pete's judgment was usually good, and he knew that the girls would be friendly and agreeable.

She shut off the Mexican music. "What is the matter, Rack?"

"Nothing."

She came and sat on the arm of his chair, and her fingers touched his cheek. "I am not an infant, Rack. I know what is troubling you. But I cannot help it."

He stirred in the chair, acutely aware of her nearness, of her faint scent. "It's all right," he said impatiently.

"No, it is not right—for you." She lowered her gaze. "Please understand. You see, my aunt in Mazatlan, who raised me and taught me dancing, she was very strict. Kind and good, but with exact rules about a young girl's behavior. Perhaps she was extra strict with me, because she feared that I might be like—like my mother. My aunt's teachings will always be with me. Can you understand—a little?"

He didn't answer, and pulled her down until she lay in

29

his arms. Her eyes were soft and her lips trembled a little. He kissed her, gently at first, and her lips grew warm. Presently his hand went to the buttons of her blouse. She stirred, and he felt her warm tears on his face. He tried to kiss her again, but she twisted away with a little moan and he let her go. She stood up and moved away, buttoning her blouse. He watched her silently as she stopped by the record player and turned it on. There was a brief silence, and then the room was filled with the soft muted melody of a Mexican love song, all guitars and whispering drums.

He got to his feet and went to her. Gently he placed his hands on her shoulders, and he felt her stiffen a little. The music floated through the room, plaintive and haunting. He didn't know what he thought or felt. Slowly she turned to face him. She brushed the back of a hand across her eyes and gave him a tremulous smile. "I am sorry, Rack, honest and truly."

He tried to smile. "Don't be. Everything's fine." He half turned and moved·to the door. "I'd better go."

"Rack . . ."

The music throbbed softly as he stepped into the hall and quietly closed the door.

Pete Davos was in bed, reading a newspaper. His short curly black hair glinted in the light and his broad naked torso was dark against the propped-up pillows. White teeth flashed as he greeted Ramsey. "Hi, pal." He glanced at a watch strapped to a hairy wrist. "Only two o'clock. You're early."

"Yes," Ramsey said shortly. "Simpson gone to bed?"

"Yep. He spent the whole day buying supplies and getting things lined up. I guess all we're waiting for now is our dough from Pittsburgh." Pete crossed his arms behind his head. "Think of that mahogany, Rack. I'm ready to pull out tonight."

Ramsey grinned at him. "Real anxious, huh?"

"Sure. What about you?"

Ramsey didn't answer and started to undress.

Pete said suspiciously, "You're not gonna back out on us, are you? Because of that girl? Sara?"

"Hell, no." Ramsey entered the closet and hung up his suit. "We'd better give notice to the boss tomorrow."

"I already did," Pete said, grinning. "Tomorrow's our last day on the job. We can pick up our checks on Monday.

30

The boss was a little sore at first—we didn't even work long enough to join the union. But he said if we're ever back this way, he'll hire us again."

Ramsey came out of the closet naked. He was built like a fullback or a heavyweight fighter. There was no fat on him and the muscles moved smoothly beneath the skin. As he went to his bed, he asked, "What about those women you lined up for tomorrow night?"

Pete sighed. "Simpson wasn't interested, and I don't know what I'm going to do with two of 'em. One is a cute little black-haired number. The other is too tall for me, but, boy, is she stacked. A redhead."

"Still want me to go along?"

Pete gave Ramsey a puzzled look. "I thought you was all tied up with Sara?"

"Not tomorrow night."

"You have a fight with her or what?"

"No."

"I don't get it," Pete said. "You been with her every night this week, and all of a sudden——"

"Shut up," Ramsey snapped, "and turn off that goddamned light."

The light went out and Ramsey heard Pete chuckle in the darkness.

CHAPTER 5

SUNDAY NOON Ramsey opened his eyes to bright sunlight. His head pounded wickedly and his mouth was hot and dry. He squinted his eyes against the sun and tried to remember all that had happened the night before.

He and Pete had met the girls on a gulf pier where there'd been a huge dance floor and a brassy big-name band. His girl had been a redhead, all right, as Pete had said, with a short freckled nose, big blue eyes and a generous red mouth. He remembered the feel of her tall body against him as they danced, and the friendly throaty sound of her laughter. Pete's girl had been small and dark-eyed.

Her name was Arletta. The redhead was Leona. Just a couple of thirsty and healthy girls out for a good time, as he and Pete had been. A mutually enjoyable evening.

He looked across the room at Pete's bed. It was empty, and he remembered then that Pete and Arletta had drifted away some time during the night's revelry, leaving him and Leona alone. He had a hazy recollection of Leona's two-room apartment, of her warm lips and sturdy body and, later, the cool dawn breeze on his face as he walked unsteadily to the Gulf Hotel. He brought his left wrist around in front of his eyes. Twelve-thirty on a Sunday afternoon. He crawled cautiously off the bed, stood up and went to the bathroom, swaying unsteadily.

He felt a little better after he'd shaved, brushed his teeth and showered. He put on cord slacks and a short-sleeved shirt and was donning socks and loafers when Pete came in. His dark skin held a pale tinge and his eyes were red-rimmed.

"Cheers," Ramsey said. "I gather you and Arletta hit it off fine."

Pete stumbled to the bed and held his head with both hands. He groaned.

Ramsey said, "There's some aspirin in the bathroom."

"Arletta gave me some. It didn't help."

"How about a drink, pal?"

"Please," Pete pleaded. He stretched out on the bed and closed his eyes. "Go away. Let me die."

There was a soft knock on the door. "Come in," Ramsey called.

Nevil Simpson stepped into the room. He peered at them over his gold-rimmed glasses and said mildly, "Big night, boys?"

Pete groaned.

Simpson moved his head slowly from side to side and lifted a reproving finger. "Moderation in all things is the secret of a happy life. Always remember the law of physics that every action has a reaction."

"Amen," Pete mumbled, holding his head.

Simpson winked at Ramsey and said, "You have letters from Pittsburgh at the desk."

"That'll be our money," Ramsey said.

"Good. I think we can be ready to leave by Wednesday noon."

"All right."

Suddenly Ramsey thought of Sara Colvin. He knew that she didn't work on Sunday, that the Jungle Tavern was closed, and late in the afternoon he telephoned her apartment. Her soft voice answered immediately.

"Yes?"

"Hello," he said.

"Oh, Rack . . ."

"What're you doing right now?"

"Dressing, fixing my hair."

"For me? How about dinner, some quiet place? I think we should talk a little, Sara."

"Rack, I—I am sorry. I did not hear from you, and I have made another engagement . . ."

His fingers tightened on the phone. "Break it."

"I would like to, truly, but I cannot."

"All right," he said stiffly. "I'll be seeing you—maybe." He was acting badly, he knew, but he couldn't help it. What the hell was the matter with him?

"Rack, I am sorry, but—"

"Sure. So am I." He hung up.

He spent the remainder of the afternoon walking the streets aimlessly. He thought of calling the redhead, Leona, but remembered that she had told him that she had a date with a boy from Beaumont. *He's an old friend, Rack, honey, and he has a Caddie convertible, and all . . .*

At seven o'clock he had dinner with Pete and Simpson at the Gulf Hotel. Afterward they went up to the room he and Pete shared. Simpson brought a bottle of Scotch and he and Pete began a game of double solitaire. After one drink of the Scotch, Ramsey left the two men talking about Mexico and went out to a movie. When he left it, he couldn't remember what it had been about. The hotel room was dark and he heard Pete snoring gently. He undressed quietly and got into bed. Before he went to sleep, he thought, *She's with him, Blake Bowen, her employer. Does she tell him about the teachings of her aunt in Mexico . . . ?*

The next day, Monday, they pooled their cash, a little over thirty-five hundred dollars. Everything was to be share and share alike, with all expenses and the hoped-for profits split three ways. Simpson then proposed a legal partnership agreement. Ramsey and Pete protested, saying that it was not necessary, that they could trust one another. But Simpson was firm, and in the end they picked a lawyer from the telephone book. His office was close to the Gulf Hotel and his name was Jefferson W. Carr.

"A good, solid American name," Simpson said. "We shall give him our patronage."

The outer office of Jefferson W. Carr, Attorney-at-Law, consisted of paneled walls, thick tan carpeting, a few straight chairs, framed diplomas, and a pale blonde secretary behind a typewriter on a small desk. She wore heavy dark-rimmed glasses and a crisp white blouse with frilled collar and sleeves. Her nose was a trifle too long and her lips were thin but very red. She gazed at the three men with an expression of cool inquiry.

Before Nevil Simpson could speak, the door to an inner office opened and a man carrying a bulging brief case stepped out. He was stocky and a little below average height. His eyes were a frosty gray behind rimless glasses, his nose thin, and his mouth beneath a narrow black mustache was sullen-looking, with drooping corners. He wore a dark gray suit with a vest, a white shirt with a stiff collar; his tie was a sober court room gray. A gray felt hat with the brim turned up all around sat squarely on his head. His expression, at the sight of the three men, was one of faint annoyance.

Nevil Simpson said politely, "Mr. Carr?"

"Yes, but I am just leaving, as you can see." The lawyer spoke in a flat nasal voice. "I must catch a plane for Austin."

Simpson inclined his head gravely. "Very well, sir. We will see another lawyer." He nodded at Pete and Ramsey and turned to leave.

"Wait," Carr said quickly. "I have a few minutes. What do you want?"

"A partnership agreement," Simpson said, "for the three of us."

Carr took a gold watch from a vest pocket, glanced at it. "Very well," he said shortly. "I have time for that." He turned back into the office.

Simpson, Ramsey and Pete Davos followed him into a large room where a wide window overlooked the gulf. One wall was filled with thick legal volumes behind glass doors. There were chairs, but Carr did not ask them to sit down.

He sat behind a big glass-topped desk and poised a fountain pen over a ruled yellow pad, not bothering to remove his hat. "Just what sort of agreement do you want?"

Simpson told him in a quiet, precise voice, glancing occasionally at Pete and Ramsey for approval. It took twenty minutes to draw it up. Then Carr pressed a button beside his desk. The long-nosed secretary entered immediately, and he handed her the agreement. "Please type this, Miss Whitney. Three carbons." She nodded and left. Carr said to Simpson, "That will be twenty dollars."

Pete Davos whistled softly. "A buck a minute," he murmured.

"I am not charging for my time," Carr said coldly. "I am charging you for knowing how to draw up a partnership agreement."

"Very well, sir," Simpson said. "Please keep it for us. We will return in three or four months perhaps. If not, we will contact you by mail." He nodded at Ramsey. "Pay the gentleman, Rackwell."

Ramsey paid him. Carr dropped the money into a desk drawer and locked it. "Thank you," he said shortly. "Miss Whitney will have the typed copies for your signatures in a few moments. Each of you sign them in her presence. She is a notary public and will certify them. You may retain one copy, if you wish. We will keep the others on file." He stood up, lifted his brief case from the desk, and started for the outer door. He stopped abruptly.

A girl stepped into the office. Miss Whitney was behind her, looking nervous. "I told her you were busy . . ." She gnawed at the knuckle of one finger.

"Very well," Carr snapped, and Miss Whitney disappeared. Carr smiled at the girl, but his gray eyes showed annoyance. "Hello, Marcia. What brings you down here?"

The girl's gaze flicked over Ramsey, Pete and Simpson, and then back to Carr. "Did I interrupt something?" she asked lightly, moving up to Carr with a long graceful stride. "I just came to say goodbye, darling." She patted his cheek.

Watching her, Ramsey saw that she was tall and slim, with black hair combed smoothly back over small flat ears and tied with a red ribbon in back. Her eyes beneath neatly plucked black brows were big and soft brown, with heavy lashes. Her dove-gray suit clung smoothly and smartly to her slender form, accentuating the slim waist, the delicate curve of her hips and the soft swell of her breasts. A red silk scarf was knotted at her throat, bringing out the whiteness of her rather large but well-shaped mouth.

"I'm just leaving, Marcia," Carr said. "I must hurry."

"Can I drive you to the airport?" Her voice was strong and clear.

"I have my car," Carr said. "I'll leave it at the airport until I return."

"Have a nice trip, darling." She kissed him lightly, seemingly unaware of the presence of the other three men.

"Thank you," Carr said stiffly. He dabbed a handkerchief to his mouth, inspected it for lipstick stains. "I'll be back in four or five days, I hope, but you know how those legislature committee things are." He moved past her to the outer office.

The girl turned then and gazed curiously and frankly at Simpson, Pete and Ramsey. When her gaze met his, Ramsey thought he detected a sudden glint of interest. He watched for things like that. He knew, of course, that he was attractive to women, most women, anyhow, but he wasn't vain about it. He smiled at her.

She didn't smile back, but her steady cool gaze never wavered. Something like a shiver went up Ramsey's spine.

From the doorway Jefferson Carr said impatiently, "I really must go, Marcia. My plane . . ."

She blew a kiss on long slender fingers. "Run along, darling."

Carr hesitated, his expression suspicious and doubtful. Then he turned abruptly and went out, carrying the brief case. The outer door slammed behind him and the only sound was the busy typing of Miss Whitney. Then the tall girl's gaze swung slowly back to Ramsey. He was aware that Pete and Simpson were moving past him to the door, but he didn't look at them. There was a small silence. And then Miss Whitney's typing stopped and he heard her say crisply, "Sign there, please."

Ramsey didn't move. He had an odd sensation that if he looked away the girl would be gone. She was smiling a little now, her full lips barely curved, and there was a reckless light in her eyes. He wondered briefly if she had begun her afternoon drinking early, and decided that she had not. She was the cocktail-swimming pool-country club type, but for all he knew she could have been a tennis champion in training. She had that look, too.

Ramsey heard Nevil Simpson's voice, "Rackwell, will you sign this agreement, please?"

"In a minute," Ramsey said, not taking his gaze from the girl. "You go ahead. I'll see you at the hotel."

"Very well," Simpson sighed.

There was a brief silence, then the faint rustling of paper and the scratching of a pen, followed by the sound of a door opening and closing. Ramsey looked away from the girl, saw that Pete and Simpson had left the outer office. Miss Whitney, her thin mouth a red slash, began to type briskly. Ramsey swung his gaze back to the girl. She was watching him coolly, her lips still curved, almost mocking now.

"Hello," he said.

"Rackwell," she said. "That's an odd name."

"After my maternal grandfather, who fought at Bull Run. My friends call me Rack."

She nodded toward the outer office. "The man with the glasses—he called you Rackwell."

Ramsey grinned. "Simpson? He's the exception—but a friend, though."

She held out a hand. "I'm always glad to meet Jeff's clients. I'm Marcia Stockton."

Her fingers were cool and soft. He held them a little longer than necessary. Then the meaning of her name hit him, and he released her hand. "Stockton," he said. "That's a well-known name in Texas."

"My father was Clint Stockton."

"I know." Everyone knew about old Clint Stockton, he thought, one of the last of the early wildcatters who had pyramided a vast fortune. Oil money. There had even been a book written about Clint Stockton. Ramsey had read it. The old man had died two years before, leaving ten million dollars, more or less, to his only child, Marcia. And this was Marcia gazing at him with cool mocking eyes. Her left hand moved to the scarf at her throat and he saw the white glitter of the big diamond on the third finger.

She caught his glance. "Jeff and I are to be married next month," she said.

Ramsey sighed. "That's nice. All the best." He turned and moved toward the door. Even without the engagement ring, he thought, she was out of his league and he was wasting his time.

She stepped quickly past him, closed the office door and stood facing him with her back to it, the same little smile playing about her lips. Beyond the door, in the outer office, Miss Whitney's typing stopped for a shocked second. Then it began again, slowly.

Marcia Stockton said softly, "What's your hurry, Rack? Did my name and the ring scare you?"

"I'm not scared." He gazed at her steadily, waiting for her next move. He was interested but wary.

For the first time her gaze shifted from his. Black lashes lowered over white cheeks and she pressed her palms against the closed door. The invitation was unmistakable. He put his hands on her shoulders and pulled her to him roughly. A little sigh escaped her and her lips parted as they kissed. Then she pushed him away. Silently he reached for her again, but she shook her head and held him away. "No, not here." She glanced at the door. "Remember Little Miss Snoopy out there."

"To hell with her."

She came against him. Minutes later they stood apart. Coolly she applied fresh paint to her lips. "Thanks, Rack. That helped."

"Helped what?"

"The jitters I've got."

"Always glad to be of service." He grinned at her. He was sure of himself now, on familiar ground. Maybe she had ten million dollars, but she was still a woman. He said curiously, "What gave you the jitters?"

She shrugged carelessly. "Everything."

"Maybe a drink would help?"

"Maybe." She smiled. "Do you like me?"

"That's a silly question."

"You don't know anything about me."

"I know enough."

"I'm really not a very nice person."

"Neither am I," he said.

"Are you married?" she asked. "Not that it matters."

"No."

She gazed at him thoughtfully. "Now what?"

"I mentioned a drink."

"All right. In a bar—or at my place?"

38

He didn't hesitate. "Your place."

"Good." She smoothed the red scarf and touched her hair. "Do I look all right?"

"You look wonderful."

She stepped close and with a scented handkerchief wiped a corner of his mouth. "My, my," she said reprovingly. "I do believe you've been kissing someone."

"Just an old flame," he said, grinning. "Happened to meet her in a lawyer's office."

"New flame," she said, and opened the door.

Miss Whitney gazed at them coldly and handed Ramsey the copies of the partnership agreement. He signed them below the signatures of Pete and Simpson. She folded them briskly, placed them in a long envelope, sealed it and tossed it into a wire basket on the desk. Ramsey saw the typewritten words on its face: *Partnership Agreement—Simpson, Davos and Ramsey.*

Marcia Stockton said sweetly, "Good night, Miss Whitney."

Miss Whitney's thin lips barely moved. "Good night, Miss Stockton."

Marcia took Ramsey's arm and they went down to the street. She had a yellow Packard convertible at the curb beside a No Parking sign. "You drive," she said.

He got behind the wheel and they swung out into the late afternoon traffic. To Ramsey none of it seemed quite real; the yellow sunlight, the slanting shadows, the people on the streets, the cars they passed, the girl sitting quietly beside him.

"By the way," she said. "What's your last name?"

"Ramsey," he said.

"Rack Ramsey—a nice name." She moved on the seat until her thigh touched his.

CHAPTER 6

SHE LIVED IN a big white house overlooking the gulf. There were a swimming pool, a tennis court, a caretaker's cottage, a private beach and a dock, acres of lawn dotted with shrubbery, a big garage containing a Jeep and a new Buick station wagon. Ramsey parked the Packard in a curving drive beside a flagstone walk and they moved across the grass to a wind-swept terrace. The gulf stretched blue-green below them and far out against the sky two black oil tankers rolled slowly toward the harbor.

She said, "Excuse me, Rack." Her high heels clicked over the tile and she disappeared through a pair of French doors.

He sat in a deep canvas chair and gazed out over the gulf. Presently he lit a cigarette, cupping the match flame against the wind, and stretched out his long legs. There was the damp smell of salt on the wind as it whipped the smoke from his lips. He still had the feeling of unreality, but he shrugged, and wondered what Pete and Simpson were doing. He thought of Sara Colvin, too, but quickly put her out of his mind. Then he heard footsteps behind him. He stood up and turned.

Marcia Stockton, followed by a brown little Mexican maid carrying a tray of bottles, glasses and ice, was crossing the terrace toward him. The wind tugged at the red scarf at Marcia's throat and blew a strand of black hair across one cheek. She looked a little like a Mexican herself, Ramsey thought, or Spanish, maybe, with her rather high cheekbones and the dark eyes and hair contrasting with the white skin. The maid placed the tray on a low table and Marcia said, "Thank you, Theresa."

The maid gave her a shy white-toothed smile and went back into the house.

Marcia said, "How's your touch with martinis?"

"Fair. I once tended bar in Jersey City."

"You've been around a lot, haven't you?"

"A little." He mixed and stirred the cocktails and poured them into thin long-stemmed glasses. "No olives," he said. "Are you fussy about your martinis?"

"No. I guess Theresa forgot them. But, then, she only drinks tequila, and you don't want an olive in that." She sipped her drink and smiled at him. "Very good."

"Thank you, Madam." He made a slight bow.

They sat side by side and the wind swept in from the gulf and over the vast lawn and across the terrace and was cool on their faces. She looked at him in the wind and laughed. "Isn't this nice, Rack? Better than a smoky bar?"

40

He nodded, and asked, "How did you ever happen to get mixed up with a cold-blooded character like that lawyer?"

"Jeff?" She gazed at him over the rim of her glass. "Why do you ask?"

He shrugged. "He just doesn't seem to be your type."

She said mockingly, "Do you think you're my type?"

He grinned. "I'd like to try and be your type."

"I think we're two of a kind. Don't you?"

"Maybe."

"What do you do for a living?"

"A little of everything. When I work in the oil fields, I'm a rigger."

"What's a rigger?"

He gazed at her in surprise. She was Clint Stockton's daughter, and she didn't know what a rigger was, or pretended not to. He laughed. "Never mind. It's very dull work—except when you bring a well in." He took a swallow of his drink, thinking that the ten million dollars didn't make any difference. She was just a woman, smarter and more polished, maybe, than most of the women he'd known, but the money had done that.

He had the feeling that she was the kind of woman he understood, and who understood him. He thought about it seriously; she was rich and beautiful and she could have what she wanted, when she wanted it, and she may as well. Life was short and it offered so few pleasures. Some people liked kids and a home and a steady job, their work, maybe even a career, but it was not for him, or for Marcia Stockton, either, and she was right—they were two of a kind. Sara Colvin belonged to the other kind, the steady ones, and maybe Pete Davos would, too, if he had a chance, and Nevil Simpson, who wanted the mahogany so that he could re-marry his former wife, if she would have him, and settle down.

He placed his glass on the table, stood up and leaned over Marcia Stockton. She pulled him down. They kissed and part of her drink spilled to the terrace. He took the glass from her and she came up out of the chair against him and clung tightly, her cheek against his chest. He felt her tremble. "Hold me a minute, Rack."

He held her, and presently her trembling stopped and she raised her head. In the wind and the coolness they kissed again, and now her lips were warm and demanding. When they stood apart, he said, "Do you want another drink?"

She nodded, sat down again and smoothed her skirt over her knees. Her eyes were a melting brown, the mockery gone, and her parted lips held a full soft look. He handed her a glass. Her gaze shifted away from his. "Why don't you tell me about it?" he asked gently.

"About what?" Her voice was low, and still she didn't look at him.

"I suppose you pick up strange men every day?"

She looked at him then. "You make it sound—cheap."

"Cheap is not a nice word."

"It's the word for me." Her lips twisted with a faint bitterness. "Do you have any illusions, Rack?"

"Not many. I know I'm cheap, but there's nobody but me to care."

"Just a couple of heels." She lifted her glass. "Hi, brother heel. Please forget my girlish reference to illusions."

"You still haven't told me."

She drained her glass. As she held it for him to fill, she said, "It's not much. Just one of my bitchy days."

"Yes?" he said carefully.

She looked down at her glass. "I've been alone all day. It seems that I'm alone a lot lately. This morning I swam a little, wandered on the beach. After lunch I tried to take a nap, but I couldn't. I lay on my bed and thought—never mind what I thought. The house was so still, with only the sound of the wind. We always have the wind out here. I wanted to talk to somebody, anybody."

"You must have many friends," Ramsey said.

"Of course. But they bore me. The same faces, the same love affairs, the interminable silly round of cocktail parties and dinners, the same men, married mostly, who suggest quite frankly that I go to bed with them, the same dirty jokes told politely and with lifted eyebrows, all very gay and sophisticated and rotten. I loathe my friends. So I rang for Theresa. She didn't come, and I was furious. I searched the house for her. Then I went to the caretaker's cottage—she's having an affair with Juan, you know. I found them in bed. It gave me pleasure to make her get dressed and come to the house. She sobbed like mad and

42

Juan hid under the covers. It was so ridiculous, so pathetic, that I laughed. . . . I told you I felt bitchy."

"Poor Theresa and poor Juan," Ramsey said. "Maybe it's true love."

"I wouldn't know about that. Theresa should do her loving on her days off. I put her to dusting the upstairs. Then I drank some brandy. It didn't help at all. After a while I remembered that Jeff was flying to Austin this afternoon. I would go into town and say goodbye to him, I thought. It was something to do, an excuse to get out of the house. Then I saw you. . . ."

"What about that lawyer?" he asked. "Are you really going to marry him?"

"Yes. Maybe marriage is what I need. Dad always liked Jeff, and before he died he made me promise that I'd marry him. I—I loved my father, and you know how those death bed things are. I've been stalling Jeff for two years. He finally pinned me down to a wedding next month." She finished her drink. "It's what Dad wanted and I promised. I suppose he thought that faithful Jeff could look after me and the Stockton money, too."

"What do you want?"

She held out her glass. "Another drink, right now." As he filled her glass, she said, "This afternoon I was ready for —for anything. Just so it was different, and new—something to snap me out of the deadly mood I was in. When I saw you, I knew I could stop looking. It was like a—a spark, like you read in books. Crazy, isn't it?"

"Nice crazy." He was beginning to feel the drinks.

"Do you have a girl, Rack? I mean, one special girl?"

He shook his head, thinking with faint sadness of Sara Colvin.

Marcia Stockton laughed, tossing her head in the wind. Her eyes held a hot brightness, and he knew that the drinks were getting to her, too. "You're a liar, but I don't mind . . . Darling, maybe it's high time I got married."

He caught the "darling," and said, "Not to Jefferson W. Carr. What does the W stand for?"

"Webster. Jefferson Webster Carr, a solid American name."

"That's what Simpson said. We picked him from the telephone book."

"Who's Simpson?"

43

"A friend. He calls me Rackwell."

"I remember." She untied the red scarf. The wind was stronger now and the last light of the day was fading into blue dusk. The gulf was a dark rolling smoothness and the sky was a bloody-streaked curtain on the horizon. She stood up, and Ramsey stood, too. She stared at him, her face pale in the dusk. She said something, but the wind carried the words away.

"What?" he asked.

She shook her head, smiled provocatively, and moved away from him. He watched her enter the house. Then he turned and gazed out over the gulf. What the hell was he supposed to do now? How did the martini and swimming pool set handle these things? He tried to light a cigarette, but the wind was too strong, and he flung the cigarette away, turned abruptly and entered the big house. The French doors closed behind him and the sound of the wind died to a low moan.

He stood in a large red-carpeted room. A dim light in an alcove cast a soft glow over book shelves, an array of divans, chairs and polished tables. At the far end was a wide stone fireplace with a mirror above it reaching to a high beamed ceiling. He saw his shadowy image in the mirror, far away, like a figure in a Dali painting. There was a feeling of space and silence, and he felt vaguely uneasy. A carpeted hall was on his right. He moved down it to an open door with no light beyond. He moved through the door and saw the low white shape of a bed and smelled the faint fragrance. A huge pale rectangle of window revealed the dark evening sky and clouds streaking before half a moon. The wind blew through screens and stirred the edges of heavy drapes. He stood still.

Behind him she laughed softly.

He turned and saw her standing against the wall. Her body gleamed softly in the gloom and the shadows were soft on the curves and gentle hollows. She was thinner than he had thought, almost bony, but it was a smooth clean thinness. She moved to him and he reached for her and felt the velvety warmness. She made a small sound, like a child's plaintive whimper.

At midnight he left her.

44

"Don't go," she whispered drowsily. "Stay here with me."

"I'll be back."

"When?"

"In the morning."

"If you come early, I'll still be in bed."

"I'll come very early."

"Where do you live?"

"At the Gulf Hotel."

"Where is that? I never heard of it. I don't know anything about you. I want to know it all. Please stay."

"I'll see you in the morning."

"I'll be waiting." She sighed sleepily. "Take the Packard."

He paused at the bedroom door. He heard her regular soft breathing, and knew that she was already asleep. He went through the dark silent house and out to the terrace. The wind had died to a gentle breeze and the moon was high and very bright. He drove the Packard into the city, stopping once at a drive-in to eat two beef sandwiches and drink a glass of milk. He left the car in an all-night parking lot near the Gulf Hotel and went up to the room.

Pete and Nevil Simpson were playing their game of double solitaire. They gazed at him silently.

Ramsey took off his coat. "Hi," he said.

Pete said, "You got lipstick on your kisser."

Ramsey wiped his mouth with a handkerchief.

"That gal looked like class—and dough," Pete said. "Was it any good?"

"Pete," Simpson said, "don't pry into Rackwell's personal affairs."

Ignoring Simpson, Pete said, "Sara called for you tonight. I told her you was out to a movie."

"Thanks, pal," Ramsey said dryly.

"She wants you to call her. I told her you would."

"If you don't mind," Ramsey said evenly, "I'll make my own dates."

"All right, but just remember we got a date on Wednesday. Do you suppose you can tear yourself away from your women long enough to go to Mexico?"

"To hell with you." Ramsey grinned at Pete, but he felt a faint anger and resentment.

45

"You gonna go with us?" Pete stuck out his chin. "You won't back out?"

"Now, Pete, don't talk like that," Simpson said in his mild voice. "Rackwell has given his word. We are all partners now."

Pete's heavy dark face was sullen. "You don't know him like I do. Listen, I remember one time in Vegas . . ."

Ramsey entered the bath room and slammed the door.

CHAPTER 7

IN THE MORNING she was waiting for him on the terrace. She wore a thin white sweater tucked into brief tan shorts. Her black hair was tied back with a red ribbon, and her long slim legs were a pale ivory in the sunlight. She kissed him lightly and the Mexican maid, looking sleepy-eyed and weary, served them breakfast. Afterward they sat talking in low tones and drinking coffee. She told him that she had no close relatives and that her mother had died when she was sixteen. She had attended school in Connecticut, eloped with a boy from Dartmouth when she was eighteen, divorced him a year later and returned to Texas to stay with her father. Three years later her father had died.

Ramsey told her a little about himself, but he did not tell her about the impending trip to Mexico. Maybe he would tell her, and maybe he wouldn't, he thought; he would wait.

After a time, when the sun was almost directly overhead, she suggested a swim. She found some trunks for him, saying that they had belonged to her father. They fit him very well. They swam in the gulf, basked on the beach in the sun, and after lunch on the terrace he sat beside her and closed his eyes. He thought of Pete and Simpson and of their dream of a fortune in mahogany waiting for them in Mexico, and suddenly the whole project seemed absurd to him. Why had he agreed to go? Now he only wanted to stay here with Marcia, a beautiful spoiled girl

46

who knew what she wanted—and who had ten million dollars.

Beside him she whispered, "Last night, after you left, I awoke and I was lonely . . ."

In the early evening they drove along the gulf and had dinner at a little inn high on a plain. It was late when they started back for the city through the flat lonely country with the gulf rolling darkly beyond the breakwater. Ramsey was uneasy. This was the last night, he thought, and if he were going to tell her about the Mexican venture, he should do it now. When he saw the lights of the city curving along the gulf, he made up his mind. The headlights picked up a narrow lane leading down to the beach. He slowed and swung into the lane. Marcia made no comment. The lane was narrow, rutted and sandy, and the Packard rolled gently. He stopped on a little rise slanting down to a small cove and shut off the motor. The gulf stretched out before them in the dim moonlight and slow waves lapped on the sand. Behind them on the highway the sound of passing cars was a faraway hum in the night.

He told her quickly about Pete and Simpson and the trip to Mexico, and ended by saying, "We leave tomorrow at noon."

"Oh, no, Rack."

"I can't back out now. They're my friends, and I've promised."

"But it—it's silly."

"Maybe. I can't help it."

"Why didn't you tell me before? Before we—we got to know each other?"

"I'll be back."

"How do I know?" she said in a strange hard voice.

"I promise."

"Just when will you be back?"

"Three months, maybe four."

"Lovely," she said bitterly. "That's just lovely.

"It isn't so long." He was surprised at her sudden hardness.

"It's forever," she said, biting the words, "for me. Do you understand."

"I made a deal," he said stubbornly.

"You're a fool."

47

"Listen," he said angrily, "the plans were made before I met you. And I didn't have to tell you at all, you know."

"Why bother, then?" Her voice was ugly. "Why didn't you just sneak away—with your conquering male memories?"

He reached for the ignition key. Her hand on his arm stopped him. "I—I'm sorry, Rack. I told you I wasn't a very nice person. But it—it was such a shock, and I'll miss you. Forgive me, Rack."

He didn't speak.

"But you don't have to go, not really," she whispered. "Stay with me." She came against him and pressed a cheek to his shoulder. "We'll have fun, more fun than you ever dreamed. You won't be sorry, I promise. All the men I ever knew—they are nothing now. I can't let you go, not so soon. Don't think about money. I have all we'll ever need. Stay, Rack."

"No, I can't. But I'll be back."

He felt her stiffen. "I'll be married to Jeff then," she said harshly, and moved away from him.

"You don't have to marry him."

"I will—if you don't stay with me."

"All right," he said coldly, "marry the son of a bitch."

She came back against him. "Hold me, Rack. Hold me tight." She was trembling.

He put an arm around her and he thought bitterly that he would never meet a girl like her again, not a girl with her looks and her money, not down through the years of his life. He thought of the jobs he'd had, the places he'd slept, of the meals he'd sometimes missed. And now for the first time he had a golden opportunity to settle down, to stop moving in an aimless quest for something he didn't even know he wanted. But Simpson and his damned mahogany, and Pete—they had trapped him.

"All right," Marcia whispered. "You win, damn you. I —I'll be here when you return—if you want me."

He felt a vast relief, but he said cautiously, "What about Jefferson Carr?"

"I'll tell him right away. I'll call him in Austin."

"And your promise to your father?"

She sighed and pressed against him. "I—I can't be expected to keep a promise like that—can I?"

"No," he said bleakly. "Nobody will blame you."

48

"Rack, you don't have to worry about Jeff—or anybody. I'll wait, Rack. I'll try . . ."

It was almost noon when she drove him to the Gulf Hotel. She didn't speak and stared straight ahead, her hands tight on the wheel, her eyes big and dark against her pale face. Nevil Simpson's battered Ford station wagon was at the curb before the hotel, the rear end already loaded with luggage, supplies and equipment. Simpson sat behind the wheel, smoking his pipe. Pete Davos stood on the sidewalk, his dark gaze swinging up and down the street.

She stopped the Packard across the street and Ramsey opened the door. "Would you like to meet them?" he asked her.

She shook her head quickly. "No. I hate them."

"Goodbye," he said gently.

There were tears in her eyes and her lips trembled. "Come back to me, Rack."

"I will."

"And be—be careful."

"Don't worry." He leaned forward and kissed her quickly, aware that both Pete and Simpson were now watching them silently. Then he got out and closed the door. He had a glimpse of her profile, white teeth biting at a red lower lip, eyes blinking to keep back the tears, and then she was gone with a high whine of the automatic transmission. He watched her turn a corner at a dangerous speed, and then he walked across the street.

Simpson smiled and waved his pipe in greeting. Pete's expression was sullen. "Glad you could make it," he sneered.

Ramsey nodded at the station wagon. "Is my stuff in there?"

"We packed for you—and paid the hotel bill," Pete said. "We took a chance that you'd be here."

"Thanks," Ramsey said.

"She came to the hotel this morning," Pete said, "looking for you."

'Who?"

"You know who, lover boy. Your other girl—Sara."

"That so?" Ramsey said carelessly. He felt a sudden pang of regret, of something, but he smiled.

49

"Yes, that's so," Pete said in a mincing falsetto voice. His black brows came together in a scowl. "You might at least have said goodbye to her."

"I didn't have time."

"I bet not." Pete spat into the gutter.

Nevil Simpson said mildly, "We're glad you're here, Rackwell. Everything is aboard. Are you ready to leave?"

"Sure." Ramsey turned to Pete. "We still pals, you goddamned wop?"

Pete's black expression softened a bit. "Sure, but, well —I felt kind of sorry for her. She—"

"Come on, pal." Ramsey grinned and jabbed a fist lightly against Pete's chin. "I'll buy you a drink the first stop we make."

CHAPTER 8

THEY CROSSED the Border at Brownsville and drove south to Cuidad Mante where Route 170 swung southward toward Tampico, and eventually they left the main highway and jounced over a narrow rutted road, stopping frequently while Simpson consulted a hand-drawn map. Somewhere in the state of San Luis Potosi the road ended at a dry creek bed beside an adobe hut occupied by an old Mexican couple. Simpson spoke fairly fluent Spanish and by promising the couple some pesos, which he displayed, he secured their voluble and eager assurance that they would guard the station wagon with their lives until the party returned. Simpson then gave them some cigarettes and chocolate, as a sort of down payment for the car-watching, and the three men shouldered their packs and began their journey.

For a time it was easy going over the crests on rolling hills, but when they began the descent into the lowlands they spent as much as a day hacking a mile's progress through the thick underbrush. Day followed day, and at night they slept exhausted. Each evening Nevil Simpson hunched over his maps by the fire, made notes of the day's progress, slapped at mosquitoes and sometimes talked softly to himself.

At noon of the twenty-sixth day, in a clearing somewhere south of the Rio Verde, Simpson suddenly stopped and pointed a finger. "There," he said quietly. "There is our mahogany."

At the far edge of a grassy slope it stretched out before them, a seemingly endless forest of strong, thick-trunked trees, many of them seventy to eighty feet tall, as Simpson had said. The reddish scaly bark glinted in the sun and the ash-like leaves tossed in a gentle breeze against the hot blue sky. As they stood there, the sound of the leaves and the branches in the wind was like faint organ music. Pete and Ramsey dropped their packs and stared silently. Simpson took a deep breath and gazed at the forest with a glint of tears in his blue eyes.

"My God," Pete breathed, his dark eyes shining, "there's enough wood there for all the bars on Third Avenue."

"And then some." Ramsey lit a cigarette with a trembling hand.

"If we can just find a way to get it out," Simpson said.

"Hell," Ramsey told him, "bring in a bulldozer, strip out an airfield and fly it out."

Simpson nodded slowly, filling his pipe. "That would be the expensive way, Rackwell. A road to the river would be cheaper and better. But we'll see."

Pete Davos moved away from them through the high grass. "I want to touch them beautiful trees."

Simpson squatted on his heels, puffed his pipe, and began to leaf through his note book. Ramsey peered over the geologist's shoulder. Simpson placed a finger at a spot on a penciled map and said thoughtfully, "We could establish a base camp there, and map the surrounding country. The river is north of here, and if there isn't too much swamp—"

A hoarse cry cut off his words. Their heads jerked up. Pete Davos, twenty yards away, was leaping backward in the high grass, and they caught an ugly glimpse of a huge snake's writhing coils as Pete tried frantically to shake the fangs from his wrist. Simpson cursed savagely and ran forward, drawing his revolver. Ramsey plunged after him. Simpson stopped close to Pete, aimed carefully and fired. The flat report echoed through the forest of mahogany. Simpson fired twice more, and then leaped forward, put an arm around Pete and dragged him away, out of the tall grass. Behind them Ramsey saw the snake and he emptied his own gun into the twisting dusty coils before he ran to the knoll where Simpson had laid Pete on the ground.

Pete's eyes were bright with shock. "J-Jesus," he chattered. "I—I was watching the trees, and I didn't see the damned thing . . ." Sweat dripped from his suddenly pale face.

Simpson ripped open a pack, took out the snake bite kit, and worked like a madman as he applied a tourniquet to Pete's arm. "Serum," he snapped at Ramsey.

Ramsey handed the needle over. Simpson used it with a sure and steady hand, but they both knew, as they watched Pete's stiffening body, that nothing could help him now. Silently, and with tears stinging his eyes, Ramsey cursed the mahogany and all the events that had led the three of them here to this lonely spot in an evil and forgotten section of Mexico.

Both men worked feverishly, taking turns at sucking the two punctures in Pete's wrist, and tightening the tourniquet around his already swollen and bluish arm. Once Simpson's haggard bearded face turned briefly up to Ramsey with a sad hopeless expression, but they worked on, even when Pete began to scream in pain and delirium. At sundown the rigid tormented body relaxed at last and the eyes went still and seemed to stare at them reproachfully.

Ramsey turned away, feeling sick and a bitter helpless rage. He began to sob, and he felt Simpson's hand on his shoulder. After a while, when the sun was completely gone and the mosquitoes began to sing, Simpson wrapped Pete's body in a blanket. Ramsey built a fire, his eyes avoiding the blanketed figure, and in the gloom he sat by the fire with Simpson.

"Rackwell," Simpson said softly, "I've been saving a bottle in my pack."

"Get it out."

They passed the bottle back and forth silently, and presently Simpson said, "Fer-de-lance. Snakes don't come any deadlier. Pete didn't have a chance. One of the fangs punctured a vein."

Ramsey choked on the hot whisky and said in a strained voice, "It's a damned high price to pay for mahogany."

Simpson nodded slowly, his face gaunt and hollow in the firelight. "I'm sorry, Rackwell."

"Sorry?" Ramsey said bitterly. "That's a big help."

Simpson said nothing and gazed into the fire.

"It was your idea," Ramsey said. "You and your god-damned mahogany, and a wife who won't have you." He drank again and held the bottle, not passing it to Simpson. "But you needed the money, so she'd take you back. You used Pete and me, and now Pete's dead."

Simpson hugged his knees, a haunted look in his eyes. "I'm lonely, Rackwell, and not young any more. She's all I have. I wrote her about the mahogany. She wrote back, promising nothing, but between the lines I saw that if I could give her anything approaching security, with no more moving all over the world, she would have me again." He looked at Ramsey in the firelight. "You and Pete had a chance to—to profit also. You can still profit . . ."

Something ugly flared in Ramsey's eyes. He half rose and struck Simpson on the jaw with his fist. Simpson toppled sideways and lay still. Ramsey lifted the bottle with a trembling hand and drank deeply. Then he knelt beside Simpson. The geologist stirred and opened his eyes. He looked up at Ramsey and said distinctly, "I told you it was a gamble."

"Yes," Ramsey said thickly. "To hell with it." He put an arm beneath Simpson's shoulders and pulled him to a sitting position. "I'm sorry I hit you."

"It's all right, Rackwell." Simpson's lean fingers touched his jaw. "Drink the whisky. And sleep."

Ramsey stood erect and drained the bottle.

In the morning they dug a deep oblong hole. It took them a long time. When it was ready, they lowered Pete's body gently, shoveled in the dirt and piled rocks on top. Ramsey made a crude cross from a thick branch of mahogany, carved Pete's name on it, and the date, and wedged it into the rocks. Then he stood with his head bowed while Simpson said a prayer, a gentle-voiced composite of all the burial services he had ever heard. The words drifted out over the singing of the wind in the mahogany forest: *In my Father's house there are many mansions . . . Twilight and evening star and one clear call for me . . . This is not the end, but the beginning . . . Ashes to ashes and dust to dust . . . Peter Anthony Davos, age thirty years . . . A good man and a true friend . . . May God have mercy on his soul . . . Amen.*

For a week they scouted, explored and ranged far from their camp on the knoll. On the eighth night, as they sat by the fire, Simpson said, "I'm afraid it's hopeless, Rackwell. A road to the river is impractical—too much swamp. I guess you were right about the air strip, but it will take organization and money, lots of money." He thudded a fist softly against a palm. "We've got the mahogany—but we can't handle it alone."

"You can shove the mahogany," Ramsey said.

"We're still partners," Simpson said stubbornly. "I won't stop now. You and I can still make a fortune."

"To hell with it." Ramsey tossed a cigarette into the fire and stood up. "I'm turning in."

In the morning they packed up, and after a final silent look at Pete Davos' grave they began the slow trip back. On the twenty-first day Simpson came down with malaria and they were forced to camp. The quinine ran out and so did the food. In the end Ramsey pushed on, carrying Simpson on his back. By the time he staggered up to the adobe hut where they'd left the station wagon, Simpson was babbling like an idiot.

The old Mexican couple knew about malaria, and the woman took charge of Simpson. Ramsey ate and slept and sat in the sun talking to the old man with gestures and garbled patois. After a while, when Ramsey had lost all track of time, the malaria left Simpson's thin body, and in a week he was able to travel. They gave money to the Mexican couple, more than they could afford, and Simpson thanked them gravely. The old man swung his greasy sombrero in a courtly gesture while the woman greedily counted the money. As they drove away, with Ramsey at the wheel, the old man's farewell came to them through the clouds of dust: *Adios, senors, adios . . .*

At the post office in Tampico there was a letter waiting for Ramsey and one for Simpson. They went back to the car before they opened them. Ramsey's envelope was a dainty pale blue, smelling faintly of sandalwood, with Marcia Stockton's engraved address on the flap. Simpson's was plain and white, the address penned in blue ink in a slanting backhand. Ramsey grinned at Simpson. "Go ahead. Read yours first."

Simpson tore open the envelope with a trembling hand and quickly scanned the enclosed page. Then he folded it and sighed. "She wishes me luck, and she hopes I brought plenty of quinine. I had malaria before, in Cuba, when she was with me. She hopes I find the mahogany, if that is what I want, and she—she says if I find it she will come back to me, if I promise to stay in one place. The mahogany means nothing to her, but she knows what it means to me and she hopes that our venture will be successful, because she—" Simpson gave Ramsey a bleak, sad smile. "Because she knows that I am like Lancelot, searching for the Grail." He sighed. "Angeline was always, well, romantic."

"I see," Ramsey said, gazing at the letter in his hand.

"She wrote it three months ago," Simpson said, "thinking that it would reach me before we left. Read your letter, Rackwell."

Because of Simpson, Ramsey had suppressed his feeling of anticipation and pleasure at the letter from Marcia. Now he opened it and read eagerly.

Dearest Rack: Please try hard to forgive me. It happened too fast, whatever it was that happened to us. I am married to Jeff Carr. You see, I promised my father, and I'm afraid I'm not the waiting kind. It was a lovely dream we had (or was it just a selfish dream of my own?), but if you had wanted the dream badly enough you shouldn't have left me, not after what we had and what you surely must know about me, and if you really wanted me, in spite of what I am. Forget me, darling, and be happy . . .

CHAPTER 9

IN A MURKY CAFE on the Tampico waterfront Ramsey was dimly aware of moving shadows and shrill music and shrill voices in an alien tongue, of dark men laughing and dark women laughing, of guitars and drums and the soft feel of warm flesh beneath silk as he danced to the music. It

55

seemed that he was swimming in a sea of white teeth, liquid dark eyes, red lips and glossy black hair, heavy breasts and wide hips and pungent perfume, and there was always the glass and the bottle and the hot taste of tequila. And somewhere in the moving sea Nevil Simpson sat alone against a moisture-beaded wall, watching him sadly. He wished that Simpson would not look so sad, and then there was the tequila again and plump soft arms around his neck, slow whispered words against his ear and warm breath on his cheek.

More tequila, and a strong red wine, and more music and more everything. Then whispered words in his ear, promising him paradise, and at last the cool air of the dawn and the rough dew-wet cobblestones beneath his stumbling feet, the steadying arm about him and a hot moist hand in his, the perfume and the low words. "I am good, *amigo*. I am hot like hell. You will see."

Then a dark stairway and a room smelling of sweat and old cooking, and a bed with surprisingly cool sheets, and warm nakedness beside him, full and ripe and smothering, and hands moving over him as the red glow of sunrise crept into the room. But he was beyond desire, beyond feeling. He thought fuzzily of Marcia, of Pete Davos, and all he wanted was to sleep, to forget. He muttered and pushed the girl roughly away.

At noon he awoke, instantly aware of the pounding pain above his eyes and the hot dry bitter taste in his mouth. A girl sat naked in a chair by the window, watching him, a cup half raised to her thick red lips. He smelled the hot coffee and came close to retching. The girl was broad-faced, swarthy, with heavy sagging breasts, thick thighs and flat spread-toed feet. She came to him and placed a hand on his cheek. "I have waited all the morning," she said in English. "Do you wish me now?"

He brushed her hand away, struggled off the bed and stood swaying, fumbling at a hip pocket. His wallet was still there, and he grunted in surprise. He tossed some bills to a table and lurched for the door. She flung the cup at him. It missed his head and shattered against the wall. He turned, staring stupidly. She hissed something obscene, spat at him, her face contorted. He felt a sudden nausea, groped blindly for the door, jerked it open and stumbled out. She was still hissing at him as he went down the narrow steps, leaning against the damp wall. He reached the cobblestoned street and stood blinking in the bright sunlight.

A gentle voice said, "Shall we go home now, Rackwell?"

"Simpson," Ramsey muttered, and as he spoke he thought it odd that he and Pete Davos had always addressed him by his last name. He added, "Nevil," but it sounded strange, and he quickly said "Simpson" again.

A hand touched his arm. "Come on," the gentle voice said, and he felt himself being pulled slowly along the street. "I have been waiting for you, Rackwell. It has been a long vigil. Do you have your wallet and money?"

"Yes."

"Good. And did the girl comfort you?"

"No—but her bed did." Ramsey began to remember.

Simpson laughed softly. Out over the harbor the sun glinted brightly on the water and etched the outlines of masts and funnels against the blue sky. Ramsey walked beside Simpson, and presently they were standing before their hotel. "Sleep some more, Rackwell," Simpson said, "and rest. I'll see you at dinner time."

Ramsey's muddled brain was clearing. "Why did you wait for me?"

"It's just the two of us now."

"You can have my share," Ramsey said. "Keep your goddamned mahogany."

"We are partners," Simpson said. "You carried me on your back when I was sick."

"Forget it." Ramsey smiled and touched Simpson's arm. "Thanks for riding herd on me last night." He left the geologist standing in the sun and entered the hotel.

The letter was on the dresser in his room. He read it once more, then carefully folded it and placed it in his wallet. After a bath in an ancient metal tub he stretched out on the bed. Presently he slept. When he awoke, Simpson was sitting by the window. "It is almost evening, Rackwell."

Ramsey stretched and yawned. He felt rested and he was hungry. As he dressed, Simpson said, "What are your plans?"

Ramsey shrugged. "Back to the oil fields, I guess. What about you?"

"Stay here—for a while. By the way, I reported Pete's

57

death to the police. They want your signature as a witness."

Ramsey nodded, buttoning his shirt.

"I landed a job today with an American oil company," Simpson said. "It will give me a chance to work on the mohogany thing. I have already made some contacts, and I admit that it seems hopeless. The cost would be too great, they say—too much of a gamble. But they haven't seen the mahogany, and I don't want to take anyone to it until a contract is signed."

Before they left the room, they divided their remaining money three ways. Simpson agreed to send Pete Davos' share to the sister in Saginaw, and to write her telling how Pete died. Then they went down and had dinner.

At noon the next day they had a last drink together in a waterfront bar while they waited for Ramsey's ship to sail. Simpson said, "Let me know where I can reach you."

"I'll be at the Gulf Hotel. If I pull out, I'll leave a forwarding address."

"Maybe you'd better see that lawyer—Carr, is that it? —and have him change the agreement. You can mail it to me here for my signature."

"All right," Ramsey said, "if you want it that way. But I told you—"

"It's just you and me now," Simpson broke in. "Share and share alike."

Ramsey shrugged. They went out to the dock and shook hands by the iron gate leading to the pier. "Goodbye, Rackwell, and good luck."

"Goodbye." Ramsey moved through the gate and out to the waiting ship.

During the voyage up the Gulf he got into a dice game with some soldiers bound for Corpus Christi and when he walked off the dock in Texas there were only eighty-four dollars left in his wallet. But he didn't worry about it. A good derrick rigger could always find work in oil country. He went straight to the Gulf Hotel, registered, shaved, showered, changed his clothes and then walked to the office of Jefferson Carr. It was four o'clock in the afternoon.

The prim-mouthed Miss Whitney greeted him coolly, told him that Mr. Carr was busy and asked him to have a chair and wait. She returned to her typing and Ramsey waited, wondering if she remembered him. In a few minutes an elderly couple came out of Carr's office and left.

Miss Whitney entered the office and closed the door. Ramsey decided that she remembered him, and he smiled grimly. He wondered if Carr knew about his three-day affair with Marcia, who was now Carr's wife, Mrs. Jefferson Carr.

Miss Whitney came out. "Mr. Carr will see you now."

"Thanks." Ramsey stood up and moved past her into the office. Jefferson Carr sat behind his desk. He wore a tight dark blue suit and a stiff white collar. His mouth drooped petulantly beneath the narrow mustache. He didn't rise or offer to shake hands. Looking at him, Ramsey felt a sudden jealousy. He said, "Remember me?"

"Yes," Carr said shortly. "A partnership agreement—Simpson, Davos and Ramsey. You are Ramsey, I believe."

"I gave my name to your girl."

Carr gazed at the fingernails of one hand and said carefully, "You wanted to see me about the agreement?"

"What else would I want to see you about?" Ramsey had the satisfaction of seeing the lawyer's cold gray eyes shift for an instant. "I want a new agreement drawn up. Davos is dead."

Carr looked up. "Dead?"

"A snake bit him. Never mind the details. It's just Simpson and me now."

"Is Simpson here?"

"No. He stayed in Mexico."

"I see. Was your—ah—venture successful?"

"No. We lost our shirts."

"In that case, I fail to see why you want the agreement continued."

"It's Simpson's idea." Carr had not invited him, but Ramsey sat down in a deep leather chair opposite the desk and lit a cigarette.

Carr looked annoyed. He said, "So your partner stayed in Mexico. Why did you come back here, to this city?"

Ramsey smiled without humor. So Carr did know about his brief interlude with Marcia. He said easily, "I·like this town—and Simpson wanted me to see you about the agreement."

"That could have been arranged by mail," Carr said coldly, "and Simpson will have to sign it."

"I'll mail it to him. Send the new agreement to me at the Gulf Hotel."

"Very well."

Ramsey stood up. "How much?"

"Ten dollars."

Ramsey took two fives from his wallet, tossed them on the desk and turned to go.

"Uh—Ramsey," Carr said.

Ramsey paused and looked at him.

Carr was again gazing at his fingernails. "Ramsey, I—uh—know about that foolish affair you had with Marcia—with Mrs. Carr."

"Did she tell you?"

"No, but I have my sources."

"Perhaps the little Mexican maid? Or Juan, the caretaker?" Ramsey felt a malicious satisfaction that it was out in the open.

Carr's eyes were bleak and remote. "That is none of your affair. As soon as I returned from Austin, I knew what had been going on."

"But you married her anyhow?" Ramsey's eyes were mocking.

"There is no need to be insulting, Ramsey. She is my wife now."

"I know that. Marcia wrote. Her letter reached me in Tampico."

"I see," Carr said coldly. "Do you plan to be in town long?"

"Maybe." Ramsey hesitated, and then added, "It depends."

"Upon what?" Carr asked sharply.

Ramsey shrugged and gave him a tight grin. "Who knows? Maybe I'll settle down here. It's a nice town."

Carr compressed his lips. There was hate in his eyes. Ramsey wanted to laugh in his face. Then he thought of Marcia, Mrs. Jefferson Carr. Ten million dollars. Carr should be laughing at him, he thought bleakly.

Carr said curtly, "I'll send the new agreement to your hotel."

"Thanks." Ramsey went out. Miss Whitney did not look up from her typing as he moved past her.

He spent what was left of the afternoon walking restlessly around the city. He knew that he should be seeing about a job, but there was really no hurry. The seventy-four dollars he had left would keep him for a while. He was lonely without Pete Davos, and he thought with sadness of the grave in Mexico beside the forest of mahogany. All those years in the infantry, and then to get it from a damned snake! And suddenly he thought of Sara Colvin. He wondered if she were still dancing at the Jungle Tavern, and he had an impulse to call her. But she had no doubt left by now, he thought, maybe for California where she had wanted to go. He'd better forget about Sara and about Marcia, and find another job and another girl. Maybe he'd go back to Pittsburgh or north to Wyoming, where he'd heard they were opening some wells. Or maybe he'd return to Toledo, his home town. He didn't know. Never in his life had he felt so lonely, so at loose ends.

At six o'clock he entered a small bar and grill near the waterfront, drank a bottle of beer and ordered the house speciality of French fried shrimp. He had eaten in the place before with Pete and Simpson, and the memory made him more lonely than ever. When he paid his check he talked briefly to the fat Greek behind the cash register and learned that oil field labor was still in demand. It was dusk when he left the place. He strolled the streets aimlessly, killing time, not wanting to return to his room at the Gulf Hotel.

He came to a corner and saw a familiar sign. The Jungle Tavern. He moved down to the night club and gazed at a big printed card in the window. *Three Shows Nightly, Featuring the Exotic Dancing Sensation, Miss Sara Colvin.* Her photo was there, almost life size, glossy, eye-catching. Her small slender body was clad in the scanty arrangement of colored beads and her long black hair in two thick braids over her naked shoulders. So she's still here, he thought, working for—what's his name? Bowen, Blake Bowen.

He hesitated a moment, and then pushed open the glass door and stepped into the remembered sight and sound and smell of the place. It gave him an odd feeling, like a dream dreamed over. A few couples were dancing to the music of a small stringed orchestra strumming a south sea melody. About half the tables were occupied with customers. Cigarette girls swished about in their grass skirts, and the waiters still wore white mess jackets. The tropical murals on the walls were unchanged. Ramsey left his hat with a red-lipped blonde, accepted a check, entered the bar and

61

ordered a brandy and soda. The bartender was thin and gray-haired. Ramsey didn't remember him. "What time is the next show?" Ramsey asked.

"Eight o'clock, sir."

Her schedule had been stepped up, he thought. He sipped at his drink and gazed beyond the bar to the door which he knew led to Sara Colvin's dressing room. When he had finished the drink, he slid off the stool and moved to the door.

The bartender said, "I'm sorry, sir. The gentlemen's room is that way." He nodded across the room.

"Thanks." Ramsey opened the door, stepped into a dimly-lit hall, and closed the door firmly. He waited a moment, wondering if the bartender would make a fuss about it. He didn't, and Ramsey moved down the hall. There were several doors. He stopped before one with light leaking from beneath and knocked.

A muffled voice said, "Come in."

He opened the door. She was sitting before a dressing table carefully painting her lips with a small brush. He entered, closed the door quietly, and leaned against it. Her gaze met his in the mirror and her eyes widened. She turned slowly, pulling a red silk robe up over bare shoulders. She looked the same, he thought; the same creamy skin, the same brown eyes slightly tilted at the outer corners, the same soft red mouth, and the sober little-girl look.

He smiled. "Hello, Sara."

The first surprise at seeing him was gone, and she said in her quiet voice, "Hello, Rack. I—I thought it was Blake."

He frowned. "Your boss?"

"Yes . . . You are very tanned, Rack. How are Pete and —what's his name? Simpson?"

"Simpson's fine. He stayed in Tampico. But Pete's—dead." He told her about it quickly.

When he had finished, she said soberly, "I am very sorry —truly sorry. I—I like Pete. And I am sorry for you, because he was your friend."

"The best friend I ever had."

She turned back to the mirror. "Rack, I must go on soon. Will you excuse me?"

He stepped up behind her and placed his hands on her

shoulders. Her shoulders moved beneath the silk, and he took his hands away. Their gaze met in the mirror. "Aren't you glad to see me?" he asked.

"Should I be?"

"I'm glad to see you."

"You did not even say goodbye to me."

"I know, but—"

"Did Pete tell you that I telephoned—and went to your hotel the morning you went away?"

"Yes, he told me." Her grave steady gaze in the mirror made him uneasy. "I meant to call you, Sara."

"But you did not. Why do you wish to see me now?"

He shrugged. "We had some pleasant times together."

"Yes, before you met Marcia Stockton." There was a new bitterness in her voice, and a new and strange coldness in her eyes.

"I'm sorry," he said lamely. "Can I see you tonight?"

"I'm afraid not."

"Dated up for tonight? Is that it?" He felt the beginning of anger.

"No, but it is different now, not like it was before. I cannot explain. Please go, Rack. I must dress."

"I'll be at a table out in front—in case you change your mind." He turned and left quickly, closing the door a little harder than necessary.

He secured a table for two near the dance floor and ordered another brandy and soda. Presently the room lights dimmed, a blue spot came on and the rustle of drums silenced the talking patrons. Sara Colvin glided to the floor, and the drums began to subtly increase their tempo. She moved gracefully in a wide circle, the blue spot following her, her small slender body gleaming white in contrast with the brief two-piece costume of bright beads. She danced for ten minutes, narrowing the circle, whirling and writhing faster and faster. The beating of the drums grew more savage and the only other accompaniment was a high sustained note from a reed instrument. Her face was set and serious as she concentrated on the steps of the ancient ritualistic dance. Ramsey watched closely, but she never looked toward his table. At last she sank to the floor, her head bowed, her arms and hands limp in supplication. The beat of the drums sank to a low mutter, and the sustained note of the reed became a thin whisper. Then the blue spot went off and when the lights came on she was gone. Wild applause failed to bring her back.

The orchestra began to play dance music and the small floor filled with couples. Ramsey finished his drink and lit a cigarette. Very nice, he thought, nice and accomplished and subtly sexy, taught to her by her aunt in Mazatlan, who had also taught her to be a virgin until she married. Or so she had said. All very wholesome and to hell with it. He motioned to a waiter to bring him another drink. It was then that he saw her moving through the crowd toward his table. He stood up, feeling surprise.

She had changed to a black evening gown with long sleeves and a high neck. Her glossy black hair was coiled in thick braids around her small head. Admiring glances followed her, and one shrill wolf whistle came from a wall booth where four young air force men were sitting. She came up to him, her eyes grave, seemingly oblivious of the attention she was receiving. Ramsey held a chair for her and she sat down, carefully folding the dress beneath her thighs. The remembered clean scent of her came to him as he sat down across the table and offered her a cigarette.

She shook her head.

"Drink?"

"No, Rack. Listen—"

"You were very good," he broke in. "I thought you would be in Hollywood by now."

She avoided his gaze. It—it did not work out that way. Rack, I should not be seen with you like this. Blake is away, but the waiters will tell him, and he will be angry . . ."

"To hell with Blake," he said harshly. "He doesn't own you. What is this about Blake?"

She looked at him directly. "It is a long story, Rack. Perhaps some time I will tell you. I just wanted to ask you now not to come here again, and you must not try to see me. Please, Rack." Her eyes were pleading.

"Why not?"

She sighed and glanced quickly about, almost fearfully, he thought. Something had happened since he'd last seen her, something that involved Blake Bowen. He would find out about it, he told himself, sooner or later, and he said, "I'll meet you outside tonight, after your last number."

She shook her head quickly. "No, no, you must not."

64

She stood up hurriedly. "I must go now, Rack. Goodbye."

"Wait," he said, but she was already entering the door leading back to her dressing room. He crossed the room swiftly, weaving between the tables, followed her into the hall and caught up with her at the dressing room door.

She turned. "Please, Rack, go away . . ."

"No," he said stubbornly. "Not until you tell me what this is all about."

"Rack—" She stopped abruptly as a man came out of the dressing room. He was handsome in a heavy rugged way, and Ramsey recognized him as the man who had brought Sara home the night he had waited by the hedge at her apartment. His thick reddish hair was neatly combed, and he was wearing a midnight blue tuxedo with a black tie and soft white shirt. He smiled at Sara, showing strong white teeth. His eyes were a deep blue and they held a cold sheen.

" 'Evening, Sara," he said easily, ignoring Ramsey.

"You have returned early, Blake." She shot a nervous glance at Ramsey.

"I caught a plane from San Antonio," Blake Bowen said, and added, still smiling, "Am I back too early, darling?" For the first time he glanced at Ramsey.

"Of course not." A sudden flush touched her cheeks, and she turned. "Blake, I—I would like you to meet my friend." She lifted a hand hesitantly. "Mr. Ramsey, Mr. Bowen."

Bowen nodded coolly, his eyes appraising Ramsey. He did not offer to shake hands. "Always glad to meet the customers," he said shortly, and turned to the girl, dismissing Ramsey. "Hadn't you better change for your next number?"

"Yes, Blake." She moved to the door.

"I'll see you later," Ramsey said distinctly.

She hesitated an instant, but she didn't answer or look at him. Then she entered the room and closed the door. The two men eyed each other in the dim light. Bowen was several years older than Ramsey, but they were about the same height and build.

Ramsey said, "You have a nice place here."

"Thanks. We try to run it right. Are you with a party, Mr. Ramsey?"

"I'm all alone."

"I see." Something seemed to go to sleep in Bowen's chilly blue eyes. "You mentioned that you'd see Miss Colvin later. I think you'd better forget that."

"I think not," Ramsey said.

Bowen's expression didn't change. "Nothing personal, Ramsey, I assure you. It's just a matter of policy. We prefer that our patrons do not become socially involved with the entertainment talent."

"What other entertainment do you have? Do the cigarette girls have rooms upstairs?"

Bowen's lids drooped a little, but he smiled. "No rooms upstairs," he said softly. "At least, not for the purpose you so crudely suggest."

"So Sara is your only act? She's been here almost six months. Don't you ever change your acts?"

Bowen lifted his tailored shoulders. "She's popular. The customers like her. Why should I change? I pay her well, and she's satisfied to stay here." He smiled and asked politely, "You knew her before she came here?"

"No, but I know her now. I've been away for a while, and I expect to see her tonight."

Bowen lifted one eyebrow. "Has she agreed?"

"That's none of your affair."

Bowen frowned. "I had hoped you would—cooperate."

"To hell with you."

A flame flared and died in Bowen's eyes. Then he smiled thinly and turned his back. Without knocking he opened Sara's door and stepped inside. The door closed firmly, and the click of the lock was for Ramsey's added benefit. From Blake Bowen, with contempt, for Rackwell Ramsey.

Ramsey stared at the closed door for maybe thirty seconds. When he turned away he was surprised to find that his fists were clenched and that he was trembling. He moved the short distance to the still-open door at the end of the hall, entered the bar and approached an empty stool. As he did so, a tall gray-haired man turned abruptly with a glass in his hand. He bumped into Ramsey and the drink splashed over Ramsey's coat.

The gray-haired man said instantly, "Oh, I'm sorry!" He whipped a handkerchief from the breast pocket of his blue flannel suit and began to dab at Ramsey's coat. "Very clumsy of me."

"It's all right," Ramsey said absently, still thinking of Sara Colvin and Blake Bowen. He caught the bartender's eye. "Brandy and soda, please."

CHAPTER 10

A VOICE BESIDE HIM said, "Let me pay for your drink." He turned. The tall gray-haired man in the blue flannel was smiling at him. "It's the least I can do—unless you will permit me to have your jacket cleaned." He had a smooth ruddy face, straight black brows and friendly brown eyes.

"Forget it," Ramsey said. "No harm done."

"But I insist." The gray-haired man lifted his half-filled glass. "I need a re-fill. Won't you join me?" He held out a hand. "I'm Phil Stark."

The name meant nothing to Ramsey, but he had the impression that it was expected to. He took the proffered hand. "My name's Ramsey."

The bartender brought his drink. The man named Stark drained his glass and shoved it across the bar. "The same, Orville, and let me have this gentleman's check." He leaned against the bar and said pleasantly, "Stranger in town, Ramsey?"

Ramsey smiled. "How can you tell?"

Stark laughed. He had expertly made dentures, not too even and not too white, with a few gold inlays to enhance the appearance of natural teeth. "You don't talk like Texas. You talk like Ohio, or Indiana."

"I was born in Toledo, but I haven't been back for a long time. I just came up from Tampico."

Stark cocked an eyebrow. "Oil?"

Ramsey shook his head. "Mahogany. One of my partners died, and I pulled out." He wondered why he bothered to talk about it.

Stark sighed sympathetically. The bartender brought his drink and he took a swallow. "Everything is a gamble," he said. "We keep trying to get our grubby paws on the stuff called money, and too often it eludes us. But we keep trying." He sighed again. "I do, anyhow." He hunched his shoulders over the bar and looked sideways at Ramsey. "You seem to have had a rough time. What are your plans now?"

Ramsey drank some of his brandy and soda. "I don't know. Probably get a job in the oil fields. I'm a rigger."

Stark hesitated, looked down at his glass, and then asked softly, "Must you be a rigger?" He added hastily, "Not that it isn't a first rate profession."

Ramsey took another drink. He was aware of the man named Stark beside him, but one part of his mind was still thinking of Blake Bowen entering Sara's dressing room without knocking, as if he had a right, and then locking the door. He said, "I can do a lot of things—drive a truck, run a lathe, puddle steel, tend bar, brake a freight car, swing a pick and shovel, operate a drill press, or an overhead crane—but rigging is what I really know." He paused, drank again and added, "Rigging—and how to kill men in a war."

"There are always wars," Stark said, "and always jobs for soldiers. But the pay is so small."

"Very small," Ramsey agreed, "compared to the risk."

"Yes," Stark said. "I was with an outfit at Chateau Thierry in 1918. That was fairly risky."

"So the history books say," Ramsey said.

"Oh, come now," Stark said, laughing. "I'm not so old." He stopped laughing, gazed at his glass and spoke without looking at Ramsey. "Broke?" he murmured.

Abruptly Ramsey pushed Sara and Blake Bowen out of his mind, and became warily alert. "Yes," he said evenly. "Why?" The ice clinked in the bottom of his glass as he drained it.

"I thought so," Stark said softly. His eyes were very friendly and he smiled a friendly smile. "What's your first name?"

"Rackwell." Ramsey pushed his glass across the bar and slid off the stool. On both sides of him and Stark people were drinking and talking, men and women. In the big dusky outer room there were more people listening and dancing to the softly strumming orchestra, all of them waiting for the next show when Sara Colvin would display her naked charms and perform the ancient exotic dances

68

which her aunt had taught her, among other things, in the Mexican community of Mazatlan. He moved away and said to Stark, "Thanks for the drink." ·

Stark lightly grasped his arm. "Don't be in a hurry. I want to talk to you—that's why I spilled the drink."

Ramsey frowned. "I don't get it."

"You will. Have another drink."

"No, thanks."

Stark sighed. "I was about to offer you a job."

"A job? You don't know me."

"I know more about you than you think. Sit down. Let's talk about it."

Ramsey hesitated, puzzled. Then he shrugged and got back on the stool. As Stark ordered two more drinks, Ramsey asked, "What kind of a job?"

"Don't rush me—and lower your voice."

"That kind of a job, huh?"

"We'll get to it," Stark said shortly. The drinks came and he stared thoughtfully at his glass. Then he said in a low voice, "How well do you know Sara Colvin?"

Ramsey was surprised. He said carefully, "Pretty well. I met her before I went south."

"A charming, talented and lovely girl."

"I agree. What about her?"

Stark gazed at him steadily. "I've been here for almost an hour, sitting at the end of the bar, close to the door leading back to Miss Colvin's dressing room. I come here quite often, but this is the first time I've had any luck."

Ramsey frowned. "Luck?"

"You're my luck," Stark said quietly. "When I saw Sara Colvin come to your table, I knew my luck was in. She has never sat at anyone's table, unless Blake Bowen was with her. But she sat alone with you. You talk together. She seems ill at ease. She leaves you. You follow her. Bowen comes out of her dressing room—I saw it all from here—and she seems even more ill at ease. Flustered would be a good word. I heard the conversation very clearly." He sighed. "I wish you had been more tactful, Ramsey."

"Why should I be?"

Stark said, "Blake isn't a bad sort—if you like snakes. But I always try to be tactful with him. Take my word for it—it's better that way."

Ramsey said one word, an obscene one, and drank from his glass.

"I appreciate your sentiments," Stark said. "They are aptly voiced. But it is obvious that you are slightly out of touch with conditions here at the Jungle Tavern. It is generally understood that Miss Colvin is—ah—Blake's Number One girl."

Ramsey said in a tight voice, "Meaning that there are numbers two and maybe three?"

Stark lifted his shoulders. "Naturally. Blake is a bachelor, and he plays the field. I would say that a ravishing creature named Marcia is Number Two—when her husband is out of town." He lifted an eyebrow. "I don't know about Number Three, but I assure you that Miss Colvin is Number One."

"Marcia?" Ramsey asked. "Marcia who?"

Stark eyed him silently. Then he sighed. "Perhaps I was indiscreet. Do you know anyone named Marcia?" His eyes narrowed.

"Marcia Carr? Married to a lawyer?"

Stark spoke in a suddenly flat voice. "You said you were a stranger in town."

"I met her," Ramsey said carefully, "before she was married, before I went away. Her name was Stockton then."

Stark nodded. "A famous name in Texas. Old Clint could never control her. But Jeff Carr tricked her into marrying him. He wanted the Stockton money. I hear Marcia is sick of him and has taken up with her old pals again—Blake Bowen, for one. Did you know Marcia well?"

"No," Ramsey said, feeling a sudden tightness in his throat. "So Bowen has both Sara and this Marcia on the string? And maybe Number Three? My, my." He grinned at Stark, but his throat was still tight. "All right. I've had the build-up. Does the pitch come now?"

"Not now," Stark said softly. "Not here. I gave you a friendly warning, and your reaction, generally, was satisfactory. And Sara went to your table openly, even though she was obviously fearful. That is very significant."

"Of what?" Ramsey was thinking of what Stark had told him about Marcia and Blake Bowen. And where did Sara fit in? Was she in love with Bowen?

70

"It means that Sara is attracted to you strongly. If not, she would never have risked it, even though Blake was supposed to be away. That is what I meant when I said you were my luck." Stark took a thin leather wallet from his inside coat pocket, extracted a card and handed it to Ramsey. The card was engraved and it read: *The Starlight Club— Fine Food and Liquors—Private Parties by Appointment. Phil Stark, Owner.*

"It's a little place I have. I do have a good cook and bar, but it's window dressing." Stark lowered his voice. "If you'd like some action with the dice, the wheel or cards, we can accommodate you."

"Thanks," Ramsey said dryly. "Maybe I can build up my bank roll."

"You'll get a fair play for your money." Stark took the card and with a fountain pen wrote across the face: *O.K. Stark.* "Show that to the bartender. He'll get you into the gaming room. I must be a little careful right now. There's a new reform group in power and as yet the sheriff and I haven't arrived at a mutually satisfactory financial agreement." He laughed shortly. "The new sheriff is green, but he's learning fast. . . . Shall I expect you tonight?"

"Maybe." Ramsey put the card in a coat pocket. "You mentioned a job."

"I did, indeed, but I'd rather not talk here, Ramsey. I have an appointment now, but I'll be. at the club by ten."

"All right." Ramsey had no idea what kind of a job Stark had in mind, or even if it was a legitimate job at all. Maybe he needed a croupier for a wheel, or for a dice table, or a house man for poker or black jack. Well, he thought, he'd run games before, in Vegas and other places, and the pay was about the same as well rigging. It didn't matter to him; a job was a job. Stark's approach and manner, and his reference to Sara Colvin and Marcia, puzzled him, but what had he to lose?

Stark smiled. "I'll expect you." He laid some money on the bar. "By the way, where are you staying?"

"The Gulf Hotel." Ramsey slid off the stool. "Thanks for the drinks."

"My pleasure." Stark nodded pleasantly and left.

Ramsey turned and gazed at the door beyond the bar. No one had come through it since he'd met Stark. So Blake Bowen was still with her, unless he'd gone to the upper floor by a rear stairway. Ramsey was certain that he hadn't entered the club proper. He looked at his wrist watch. Almost nine o'clock. He got his hat from the checkroom, smiled at the blonde, added a quarter to the decoy quarters in a flat metal tray, and went out to the street.

It was raining. The street glistened with water and it gurgled in the gutters. A taxi pulled up and stopped. Ramsey got in, and the driver flicked the meter lever. "The Gulf Hotel," Ramsey said.

Traffic was heavy and it took them twenty minutes. When they stopped at the hotel, Ramsey said, "Keep her ticking. I'll be right out." He ran across the sidewalk in the rain into the lobby. There was no mail in his slot, but the clerk handed him a yellow slip of paper. Typed words read: *Mr. Ramsey, Room 220, 4:40* P.M. *Call TEX 4999*. He frowned at it. The number meant nothing to him. He crossed to one of the phone booths in the lobby and dialed the number.

A soft voice said, "Hello."

He knew the voice, and the memories came back to him. Once more he was on a wind-swept terrace, and in a yellow Packard parked at the end of a lane by the water. He felt lips against his cheek and whispered words. *You don't have to worry about Jeff—or anybody . . .*

"Marcia," he said.

"Rack! When did you get back?"

"Today. . . . I got your letter."

"Rack, I'm sorry about that. I—I've missed you terribly. I—" Her voice broke.

"What's the matter?"

"Everything, Rack. It's all wrong. I should have waited for you. I—I want to see you."

His fingers tightened on the phone. "When?"

"Tonight."

He kept his voice steady. "You're married now. What about your husband?"

"Jeff's gone to Austin."

"He goes there a lot, doesn't he? That's where he was going the day I met you. Remember?"

"Yes, Rack. He has business there, clients in the state legislature. Something came up suddenly, and he called me this afternoon. . . . Come tonight, Rack. Please."

"What time?"

72

"Not early—about eleven. I must be a little careful. I think Theresa is spying on me. I'm certain that she is the one who told Jeff about us."

"And who else?" he asked with faint bitterness, thinking of Blake Bowen.

"What?"

"Never mind." What did it matter to him that she was seeing Bowen or anyone else? "How did you know I was in town and where I was staying?"

"I—I've got to go now, Rack. I'll be waiting. Goodbye." The phone clicked in his ear.

He went up to his room, got his raincoat, and returned to the waiting taxi. It was nine-thirty in the evening.

CHAPTER 11

RAMSEY COULDN'T see the gulf, but he knew it was out there in the darkness and rain. At last the taxi stopped before a low rambling structure with a small discreet neon sign which said *Starlight Club*. The black-topped parking area surrounding the place was almost filled with cars. He paid the driver, turned up his raincoat collar, ran to the entrance and pushed open a heavy oaken door. A small foyer smelled of cigarette smoke and frying foods. Just beyond was a check room. Beyond it was a bar and a large room filled with tables. From somewhere a record player was piping soft piano music into the area. A few of the tables were occupied by people eating and drinking. A tall brunette presided over the check room. She smiled at Ramsey and said in a richly modulated voice, "Check your hat and coat, sir?"

"No, thanks."

The brunette pouted prettily, and Ramsey grinned at her over his shoulder. "Sorry, honey. I'm only staying a minute." He moved to the bar.

Three brooding men and a giggling couple sat on the high stools. The bartender stood with his elbows on the bar gazing out into the dining room. He was young, with

73

smoothly combed black hair and a fresh complexion. As Ramsey went up to him, he turned his head and smiled. "Yes, sir?"

Ramsey handed him Phil Stark's card. The bartender glanced at it and nodded. "This way, sir."

Ramsey followed him around the end of the bar to a closed door. They went through this door down a carpeted passageway to another door covered with red leather and studded brass nails. A small paneled slot was set into the door about five feet from the floor. The bartender pressed a recessed button and waited silently. The panel slid back and a pair of eyes peered out. It reminded Ramsey of what he'd heard of the old speakeasy days, and of certain establishments he'd visited during and after his time in the army. The bartender held up the card for the eyes to see and said to Ramsey, "What is your name, sir?"

Ramsey told him, the bartender relayed it to the eyes, and the slot closed. Then the door opened and a fat man in a baggy brown tweed suit smiled at Ramsey. The bartender moved away. The fat man stepped aside, moved a hand in a welcoming gesture, and Ramsey entered a small foyer. The fat man opened another door, also covered with red leather and brass-studded. Behind them the first door closed with a soft click. The fat man motioned to Ramsey and they stepped into a huge room. The brightness of the lights made Ramsey blink.

Here's where the customers are, he thought, the people who owned most of the cars outside. They were standing hip to hip around dice tables and roulette wheels, sitting in groups of six to eight at poker and blackjack tables, and standing in solid array along the walls pulling the handles of slot machines. Along the far end of the room ran a long bar, and the customers were there, too, served by three busy bartenders. In the wall at one end of the bar was a barred window, with a man wearing a green eye shade behind it. A sign said *Cashier*.

White-coated waiters carrying trays of food and drinks moved among the tables, and to the people at the slot machines who were afraid to leave because they were certain that the next pull would bring up the three jackpot bars. In a large alcove were divans and deep chairs and low tables where the gamblers could relax and count their winnings, or bitterly contemplate their losses. In spite of the

74

crowd, the big room was surprisingly quiet. Even the slots whirred softly, and the other sounds were subdued; the faint deadly chuckle of the ball bouncing into the red or black on the roulette wheel, the low, monotonous voices of the croupier's calling the bets and the winners. It was serious business here. Ramsey could almost taste the intense restrained excitement and the gambling fever.

He started to move forward, but the fat man's hand touched his arm. "Just a moment," he said politely.

Ramsey looked at him. He was an amiable-looking fat man, with a round cherub face and sunny blue eyes. The eyes searched the crowd and a man detached himself from the group around one of the poker tables, as if by some unseen signal, and came toward them. Ramsey saw that it was Phil Stark.

The fat man said, "This is Mr. Ramsey. Okay?"

Stark smiled and nodded. The fat man moved away.

He doesn't look like a gambler, Ramsey thought. He looks more like a banker or a corporation lawyer, or maybe an aging actor who had once been a romantic star. Phil Stark moved his head in a slight gesture which encompassed the big room. "Name your poison."

Ramsey smiled. "No, thanks."

Stark took two blue chips from a pocket of his blue flannel jacket and offered them to Ramsey. "Here. Get twenty dollars from the cashier and try your luck with the slots."

"How tight are they?" Ramsey asked, still smiling. "Ninety per cent for the house?"

"Not quite, but close." Stark laughed softly. "Would you like a drink?"

Ramsey shook his head.

"All business, huh?"

"That's why I came here."

"Good. We'll go to my office."

Ramsey followed him through the lounge and down a short carpeted hall to a door which Stark unlocked. He flicked a light switch and they entered a fairly large oak-paneled room containing a desk of pale blond wood, red leather chairs and two tall steel filing cabinets. A small steel safe was flush in the wall behind the desk. On the wall facing the door hung small reproductions of Degas paintings. The glass desk top bore an embossed red leather

75

memorandum book, twin fountain pens in a heavy marble holder, a telephone and a pearl-handled .32 revolver.

Stark motioned Ramsey to a chair and sat down behind the desk. He saw Ramsey looking at the gun, and he said, "Paper weight."

Ramsey saw the glint of brass in the gun's cylinder. "With slugs in it."

Stark smiled thinly. "You have sharp eyes."

"Expecting trouble? A hold up—or a raid, maybe?"

Stark looked faintly annoyed. "After all, I'm not operating a hamburger stand here or a frosted malt drive-in. In every profitable business there are always risks." He paused and cleared his throat. "Do you like risks, Ramsey?"

"It depends upon the profit."

Stark smiled. "I like that. I have the feeling that we already have a meeting of minds. Would you like to make some money, real money?"

Ramsey grinned at him. "Sure, but not out there." He jerked his head toward the gaming room.

"Something a little more certain?"

Ramsey said wryly, "Yes, but I can't be too choosey, not after that mahogany deal."

Stark regarded him thoughtfully. Then he said, "Can I trust you?"

"I try to keep my word—if I give it."

"Would you keep your word—for a cut of perhaps one hundred thousand dollars?"

Ramsey kept his face composed. "How much of a cut?"

Stark sighed. "You said you weren't choosey." He hunched forward over the desk. "But it is a natural question, I suppose. I'm speaking of a ten per cent cut— roughly ten thousand dollars."

Ramsey sat quietly, hearing the echo of Stark's words. Ten thousand dollars. He felt a slow mounting excitement. "Go on," he said.

Stark opened a lower desk drawer and placed a decanter and two small glasses on the desk. An etched gold word on the decanter said *Scotch*. Stark filled a glass and pushed it across the desk. Ramsey hesitated, and then leaned forward and took the glass. Stark filled the other glass and took a slow sip. Ramsey tasted his. It was fine Scotch, smoky-tasting, smooth and hot.

76

Stark's eyes held a suppressed excitement. He said, "You will recall that I overheard your conversation with Blake Bowen this evening. It was obvious to me that you were not—not intimidated by him. That pleased me, very much. . . . May I ask a personal question?"

"Go ahead."

"Are you in love with Sara Colvin?"

Ramsey was startled but he said coolly, "Is that any of your business?"

"Yes," Stark snapped. "A hundred thousand dollars worth of my business. You must have more than a casual interest in her—judging by the way you behaved tonight."

"We're just—friends."

"I see," Stark said jeeringly. "To use a trite phrase, your relationship is purely platonic?"

Ramsey said carefully, "I didn't meet her until a week before I left for Mexico. I saw her four or five times before tonight. But what—?"

"She could be in love with you," Stark broke in smoothly, "or strongly attracted, even after such a short acquaintance. Except for Bowen, you are the only man I've ever seen her show any interest in, and I've made it my business to make certain. Oh, sometimes the customers get ideas, but she brushes them off, or Bowen has them thrown out. I think she is fond of you, perhaps more than fond—otherwise she would not have risked Bowen's displeasure, as she did tonight."

Stark paused and sipped the Scotch. "Ramsey, you're the man I need—you have come along at last." He smiled. "Your clothes are quite acceptable, you talk and handle yourself all right, and your general appearance, while rugged, is not exactly repulsive. You have already laid the ground work and, most important, you are not known around here—except by a few persons. Is that correct?"

"Yes," Ramsey said, thinking that except for Stark the only persons in the city he knew, or had met, were Marcia, Sara Colvin, Jefferson Carr and Blake Bowen.

"Good," Stark said. "A local man would never do for the job I have in mind. And when it's over, you can pull out—with ten thousand dollars." He gazed at Ramsey expectantly. "Sound all right?"

Ramsey finished his Scotch. "I'm still listening."

Stark said evenly, "Before I go any further, I must make

77

absolutely certain of one thing. If you accept this job, fine. We both shall profit. If you refuse, I want your word that you will not reveal to anyone what I am about to tell you. Do I have it?"

Ramsey hesitated only a second. Then he said, "Yes."

Stark took a deep breath. "All right. First, there is this; Blake Bowen's Jungle Tavern is merely a front for his main activity—narcotics." His eyes narrowed. "Does that shock you?"

Ramsey wasn't shocked, but he was surprised. Dope. Sara Colvin and Blake Bowen. Maybe that explained a lot of things. Beneath the surprise he felt anger—and a faint sickness. He said, "Nothing shocks me any more."

Stark's smile was faintly sad. "If you had any feelings about the girl, I extend my sympathy." He sighed. "We all must come to the end of our illusions."

"The sooner the better," Ramsey said, remembering suddenly that Marcia had used the word "illusions," too. "What is it? Heroin?"

"Mostly, I think. But he also deals in the raw morphine, marijuana, the barbiturates, anything he can get his hands on. It's big business, well organized. Only a few of us around town know about it, but we can't afford to tip the law—even if we wanted to. At least, I can't. In a way, I'm on the same side of the fence. But when I see a chance for a killing, I begin to figure the percentage. Oh, I take chances, but the dice must be talking when I do. They're talking now, through you. We can't miss—if we play it right. Will you work for me?"

"Doing what?" Ramsey said wearily. "A hi-jack job?"

"No, no. Nothing so crude." There was a hot light in Stark's eyes. "This is a lovely job, Ramsey. It merely involves making love to Sara Colvin."

Ramsey eyed Stark a moment. Then he said, "What's the catch?"

Stark spread his hands. "No catch, no gimmicks. I envy you, really, and I'd take the job myself, except that I'm married, and I want to stay in business here, and—" He smiled ruefully—"perhaps I'm a little beyond Miss Colvin's age preference." He hunched over the desk, his gaze intense. "Now, listen; for some months now it has been clear that she is the exclusive property of Blake Bowen. Everyone knows it. And he trusts her. He trusts her one hell of a lot. Last year the income tax boys and the F.B.I. gave Blake a scare. They couldn't prove tax evasion, and he slipped out from under, but now he keeps his cash in a safe deposit box in a down-town bank. He's got at least a hundred grand salted away, probably a lot more. I have ways of learning things like that." He smiled thinly. "But here's the pay-off—the deposit box is registered in Sara Colvin's name. She's covering for him, so that the money can't be traced if the heat comes on again. When he needs cash, she gets it for him—no check books, you understand? She puts the money in for him, and she takes it out when he needs it. No one but Sara Colvin can do it. Do you follow me?"

"So far," Ramsey said woodenly.

"All right. I have made a very complete study of the situation. Blake keeps very close watch on her. He sees that no men get chummy with her at the club, and he keeps tabs on her after hours. She does what he tells her to do. In spite of this, it was obvious to me tonight that she is attracted to you. I am sure that you could—ah—cultivate her." Stark's expression was faintly sly. "Do you get it?"

Ramsey said, "I make love to her, and because she loves me so damned much she double-crosses Bowen, gets his dirty money from the bank and gives it to me, with her love. Then I turn over the money to you, collect my ten thousand, and skip town."

"You put it crudely," Stark said with a grimace of distaste, "but that's the general idea. It shouldn't be diffiicult for a man with intelligence and experience. She likes you, has been closely restricted for a long time. And you could play on her sympathy—the mahogany venture cleaned you out, you need money for a new start. You could promise to take her away, even marry her—that sort of thing. The details will be up to you. It's the chance of a life time. What do you say?"

Ramsey shook his head. "I'm not that hungry yet."

Stark frowned. "I didn't think you'd be squeamish. I picked you for a man of the world. One woman, more or less, can't make much difference to you. It's dog eat dog. You know it and I know it. If you don't get that money, some one else will."

Ramsey stood up. He felt old and tired and sick at heart. "Goodbye," he said. "Thanks for nothing."

"You're a fool." Stark's voice was flat and ugly. "I

79

thought I could pick men. . . . Think it over until morning."

"I don't need to think it over."

"You're certain of that?"

"Yes." ·

"All right," Stark said harshly. "I want you out of town before morning."

"I'm afraid not," Ramsey said, "but don't worry. I won't talk."

"I can't take the chance. I've told you too much. Leave town tonight. If you don't, you'll wish you had."

Ramsey laughed at him.

"Get out," Stark said from between his teeth.

"A pleasure." Ramsey turned and left, slamming the door.

The fat man in the baggy brown suit was leaning against the wall at the end of the passageway. He was smoking a short straight-stemmed pipe, and he regarded Ramsey with friendly eyes.

· "How do you get out of this rat trap?" Ramsey snarled.

Silently the fat man turned, led him to a door, opened it and pointed with his pipe. Ramsey stepped past him into a dimly-lit garage. There was the smell of gasoline, oil and rubber. The fat man said mildly, "You and the boss have trouble?"

"No trouble. Thanks." Ramsey moved past a blue Cadillac sedan to the open garage door. Behind him he heard the inner door close softly. He stepped out into the night.

It was still raining. Cars on the highway swooshed past, their headlights bright as they rounded a curve beyond the Starlight Club. Ramsey walked swiftly across the parking area, waited for a break in the traffic, and then dashed across the highway to a brightly-lit gas station. From a booth inside he called a taxi. As he waited, he discussed the weather with the attendant and drank a luke-warm bottle of ginger ale. It was ten minutes until eleven when the taxi pulled up outside.

"Where to, Jack?" the driver asked.

Ramsey gave him Marcia's address. As they drove away, he turned in the seat and looked back. He thought he saw a car pull away from the Starlight Club, and then he lost sight of the headlights in the streaming maze of other lights. Just a customer leaving, he thought, and it didn't matter. It seemed that nothing much mattered any more.

"Nasty night," the driver said. "Off the gulf. It'll last for a week."

"Yes," Ramsey said absently. He was thinking of Phil Stark's fantastic proposition, and he wondered if Stark would find someone else for the job. He hoped not, for Sara's sake. Had she always been in cahoots with Bowen, even when he'd first met her? Did that explain her actions? Was there really a strict aunt in Mazatlan? For a fleeting instant he thought bitterly that he should have accepted Stark's offer. All that money, waiting. And he could get it, he was certain that he could. But why cut Stark in? His mind raced wildly, calculating the chances and the gain. Then he sighed and knew that he didn't want any part of it. Maybe he was cheap, as Marcia had said, but he wasn't that cheap, not yet. He would see Marcia, as she had asked, and then he would head east, or north, somewhere. But he needed money first . . .

"Along here some place?" the taxi driver asked.

Ramsey peered out of the window. Ahead he saw the curving drive leading up to Marcia's place, and through the rain was the dark outline of the big house on the hill. "Yes," he said. "The next drive."

The taxi turned, swung up the hill, and stopped before the terrace. Rain bounced and spattered on the tile and Ramsey thought of the first afternoon when he'd sat on the terrace in the wind with Marcia. Light glowed through the French doors and through the rain-streaked glass he saw a dim, slowly moving figure.

He had a date with Marcia. And Marcia had a date with death.

CHAPTER 12

THE TOE OF a dusty tan shoe nudged Ramsey's chin. He stirred feebly. The shoe nudged again, not so gently. Ramsey opened his eyes. He realized vaguely that he was sprawled on his stomach with his left cheek against a rug. He knew that Marcia was lying close to him. He could

81

smell the faint perfume of her, and he could see the smooth slim whiteness of one leg protruding gracefully from beneath the pale blue robe. The other leg was bent beneath her. Her face was turned toward him. It was empty and slack and not beautiful any more. He closed his eyes quickly, remembering. The pain in his head was almost unbearable.

Above him a soft urgent voice said, "Come on, get up. We gotta go."

Ramsey rolled on his back and squinted upward. The pain seemed to affect his vision, but he saw a hazy bulk towering over him.

"Why did you kill her?" the soft voice asked reproachfully. "Such a pretty girl."

Ramsey said something, but his voice was just a croak. All the memories were rushing back; the taxi in the rain from Phil Stark's place, his meeting with Marcia, the shot and Marcia falling, and then the blackness. "I didn't kill her," he said suddenly and distinctly.

The voice asked sadly, "What's that in your hand? A cap pistol? Come on, we can't stay here all night."

Ramsey lifted his right hand and brought it around before his eyes. He was holding a blue steel revolver tightly, one finger crooked over the trigger. He opened his fingers quickly. The gun thudded softly to the thick red rug. It lay there, a wicked blue thing, glinting in the light. He gazed upward once more. He could see better now. The man standing over him wore a brown tweed suit and the little eyes were anxious in a cherub face. The fat man from the Starlight Club.

"Come on, please," the fat man pleaded and offered a hand.

Ramsey grasped the hand and was pulled to his feet. He stood swaying, his gaze avoiding Marcia's body. It couldn't be. But he knew she was dead. The pain in his head prevented him from thinking further. Stupidly he watched the fat man stoop, drop a handkerchief over the gun, pick it up and put it in a pocket of his coat. "Looks like you're in bad trouble," the fat man said worriedly. "I followed you from the club, like Phil told me to, and I waited outside. I heard a shot and busted in, and I found you—and her." He glanced at the still body of Marcia. "Then I called Phil.

82

He wants me to bring you back to him, and that's what I'm gonna do. Let's go."

Ramsey pulled a hand down over his face. His head pounded and the world seemed to be in a fog. He felt a hand on his arm and let himself be pulled across the room. Cold wet air hit his face. He shivered, but the coldness felt good. He was moving unsteadily over the tile of the terrace, the hand firm on his arm, guiding him. A short walk over wet grass, the creak of a car door opening, the hand gently pushing him into darkness. He sat slumped in the car and he didn't protest. For the moment he didn't care. He felt numb and remote from everything he had ever known.

There was the whirring sound of a starter and the car glided down a slope and turned, gathered speed. Rain on the windshield, wipers moving, headlights approaching in the rain. A siren screamed, grew louder, filling his brain with pain. It was close, out in the rain and darkness. The headlights grew suddenly blinding and a car roared past them, toward Marcia's house, the siren a banshee's scream. From behind them there was the shriek of brakes and the squeal of tires as the car made an abrupt turn.

"The cops," the fat man muttered. "They sure got tipped off fast."

Ramsey knew dimly that a police car had passed them, coming from the direction of the city, and that it had turned into Marcia's drive. But it didn't interest him. He just wanted the pain in his head to stop. Presently it did, leaving a dull throbbing and a faint sick feeling. He sat limply, staring ahead into the rain. Marcia was dead, he thought dully. He was in a car with a fat man who worked for Phil Stark. Suddenly, through the rain, he saw the neon sign of the Starlight Club. At the same instant the car slowed.

"No," Ramsey muttered, and fumbled blindly for the door latch.

Something small and hard jabbed against his side. "Sit still," the fat man said sharply. "That's a gun."

Ramsey sat back in the seat, not caring much. His head began to hurt again and he closed his eyes. The pressure of the gun muzzle went away and the car swung off the road, circled around to the garage in the rear and came to a stop beside the blue Cadillac.

The fat man grunted as he got out. "You're awful lucky,"

he said, "to get away from back there before the law nabbed you."

"What?" Ramsey asked.

The fat man sighed. "Never mind." He walked around the car and opened the door on Ramsey's side. "Come on."

He sat in the same soft red leather chair. His head still pounded and it seemed that he was looking at things through a dim shimmering light. He blinked his eyes. The shimmering was still there, but he knew where he was. The pearl-handled .32 was still on the top of the desk. A man sat behind the desk. Ramsey rubbed his eyes and Phil Stark came into focus. Stark was reading something. Ramsey squinted and peered. A letter, a single sheet of pale blue paper with dark creases in it, because he'd carried it folded in his wallet. Marcia's letter, written to him at Tampico, telling him that she'd married Jefferson Carr.

He started to push himself up out of the chair. "Hey . . ."

Stark looked up from the letter. "Sit still," he snapped.

Ramsey sank back, trembling. There was sweat on his face. He felt weak.

Stark tapped the letter and said coldly, "A nasty business. No wonder you refused my proposition—you had murder on your mind." He opened a desk drawer and took out an object wrapped in a handkerchief. "We have your gun here, the gun you used to kill Mrs. Carr. It will bear your fingerprints. She jilted you for Jeff Carr while you were away—her letter makes that clear—and you came back and killed her. Jealousy is your motive."

It seemed to Ramsey that Stark was a long way off, far away behind the big desk. And the shimmering started again. He closed his eyes. "No," he whispered, but no one heard him.

"But you were very lucky," he heard Stark say. "For the moment you are safe, thanks to Victor. The police will not immediately connect you with the shooting of Mrs. Carr —but it would be very different if they had the murder gun, with your prints on it, and the letter. The gun alone is enough, but the letter provides a definite motive and makes it air-tight. . . . Can you hear me, Ramsey?"

"Yes," Ramsey said hoarsely, "listen . . ."

"Fortunately for you," Stark said in the same cold voice, "I asked Victor to follow you when you left here. Otherwise, you would now be in the hands of the police. I had Victor follow you because I wanted to know where you went, whom you talked to. I had revealed some very confidential information to you, and I was merely attempting to protect myself. You see?"

The shimmering haze seemed to be dissolving at last and Phil Stark was very close and everything in the office was suddenly bright and clear. Ramsey's head still throbbed, but he was no longer trembling. He felt suddenly cold as he realized the full meaning of what Stark had told him. He heard his voice say, "I didn't kill her. Somebody was hiding in the adjoining room. They shot her, while I was talking to her."

"You're grasping at straws," Stark sneered. "Who was hiding there?"

Ramsey shook his head, like a swimmer trying to get water out of his ears, and he tried to recall the details of that last shattering second. But all he could remember was Marcia, and the way she had looked when the bullet struck her face. "I—I don't know," he stammered. "We were talking, and—and I heard the shot. And then I was slugged. When I came around, your man was there, Johnny on the spot—what's his name?"

"Victor," Stark said. "But he didn't slug you and he didn't shoot anyone." He paused and said irritably, "Why don't you admit the truth? It will be much better that way."

"I've told you the truth."

Stark shrugged. "All right. It's up to you. If I give the police your gun and the incriminating letter, you will be immediately arrested for murder."

Ramsey sighed. "I see. A frame."

Stark lifted a hand. "Now, now," he said reprovingly, "there is no need to talk like that. Victor and I were merely trying to help you." He smiled. "Would you like a drink?"

"No."

Stark's gray eyes held an amused light. "Think over what I have told you. You will recall that earlier this evening you and I discussed a business proposition. I made a fair offer, but you chose to refuse it. At this time I am willing to renew the offer. Perhaps you are interested now?"

Ramsey started to speak, but he stopped. He felt lonely

85

and scared and trapped, and he wished that he'd stayed in Tampico with Nevil Simpson.

Stark said softly, "Would you like to think it over a little? If you wish, Victor and I will leave."

Ramsey stirred and glanced over his shoulder. The fat man was leaning against the wall beside the door, his pipe in his mouth, his eyes sleepy and withdrawn. It gave Ramsey a small shock to see him there; he had assumed that he and Stark had been alone. He turned back in the chair. Ten thousand dollars, he thought, would get him a long way from Texas. And he really had no choice. He spoke in a strained voice, ashamed that he could not meet Stark's amused gaze. "I still get my ten per cent?" he asked.

"I'm afraid not," Stark said, not unkindly. "Not quite. The terms have altered slightly since our first discussion. Due to the recent—ah—developments, your share is now five per cent. Of course, you will still get the gun and the letter. I'm sure you realize that those two articles will more than compensate for the additional five per cent."

Ramsey met Stark's gaze directly. "What if I just tell you to go to hell and walk out of here?"

Stark lifted his shoulders. "That would be very foolish. I would merely turn over the gun and letter to the police. And Victor is a witness."

"A complete frame job?"

Stark's lips twisted in annoyance. "Why do you keep harping on that? You killed her, didn't you?"

"No. You know damn well—" Ramsey stopped as he saw Stark's expression of tolerant amusement. He sank back in the chair, aware that he was trembling. Stark had the whip, and he was cracking it.

"Please continue," Stark urged gently. "Talk about it. If you didn't kill her, tell us who did. We're interested." He cocked an eyebrow at the fat man. "Aren't we, Victor?"

Victor didn't answer, but Ramsey saw Stark wink and he had no doubt that behind him Victor winked back, broadly.

Ramsey hesitated. Then he said, "When do I start?"

"Tonight," Stark said quickly. "Now. The sooner the better."

"What if I can't do it? Talk her out of the money?"

"You can only try." Stark grinned with a suggestion of lewdness. "It should be enjoyable work—extremely so."

He winked again, this time for Ramsey alone. "However, if you fail, if Miss Colvin does not succumb to your—ah—charms, well, you will just leave town, and no harm done." He made a dusting motion with his hands.

"But I still get the gun and letter?"

"Don't be naive. Of course not. If you fail, I will keep them as—as security. After all, you might return some day. Surely you can appreciate my position?"

Ramsey pushed himself up from the chair. His head still ached and his knees felt weak, but he stood steadily. "Do I get paid for my time?" he asked bitterly. "Do I punch a clock?"

Stark smiled up at him, hands clasped beneath his chin. "Certainly you will be paid. I don't ask people to work for me for nothing."

"How much?"

"Oh, maybe a hundred dollars or so," Stark said carelessly. "Do you need some expense money in advance?"

"Yes."

Stark opened a desk drawer, took out two fifty dollar bills and handed them to Ramsey. "If you should need more, let me know. You will want to wine and dine her in proper style. There is just one restriction—if you get into any sort of trouble whatsoever, don't expect any help from me. I don't know you, I never saw you before. Is that clear?"

"Perfectly," Ramsey said. "I do a nasty job, take all the risks, and you collect."

Stark said sharply, "Perhaps you would prefer a murder charge?"

Ramsey turned away, pocketing the money, and moved to the door. He felt numb. Behind him he heard Stark say, "Victor will drive you wherever you wish to go."

The fat man went out ahead of him. In the murkiness of the garage with the rain drumming down beyond the open door, Ramsey heard a voice behind him.

"Ramsey," the voice called softly.

He turned. The trim outline of Phil Stark was in the door to the passageway. "Good luck—Romeo," he said, and he chuckled.

Ramsey waited a second until he could control his voice. Then he said, "I'll do the job, and I'll collect the five thousand. But some day—"

Stark's laugh cut him off and the door closed.

The fat man opened the door of the car parked beside the blue Cadillac. For the first time Ramsey saw that it was a new Ford station wagon, two-tone, blue and gray. "Where to?" the fat man asked. The smell of his pipe was like rich incense.

"You smoke fancy tobacco," Ramsey said.

"Phil gave it to me for my birthday," the fat man said seriously. "He gives all of us birthday presents, a swell guy. This tobacco is Turkish, blended with—"

"Never mind. It smells like a Cuban whorehouse on Saturday night." Ramsey got into the Ford. "Take me to the Gulf Hotel."

CHAPTER 13

As RAMSEY GOT out of the station wagon in front of the Gulf Hotel, the fat man named Victor said, "Good luck."

Ramsey turned angrily, remembering Phil Stark's parting goad, but he saw nothing but solemn concern in Victor's eyes. "Thanks," he said shortly, turned and entered the hotel. He stopped at the desk, but there was no mail or any message for him. He smiled grimly, wondering what he had expected. The last message had been from Marcia, and there would be no more messages from her—unless her ghost haunted him. And that wasn't funny, he thought, as he went up to his room. Nothing was funny. How long had it been since he'd laughed?

In the bathroom he inspected the small lump behind his left ear. It was very tender, but the skin wasn't broken. He bathed it carefully with cold water. Then he swallowed two aspirin tablets, took a shower, decided to skip shaving until morning, and got out clean underwear, shirt and socks. As he dressed, he had the odd sensation that he was someone else, not Rackwell Ramsey, ex-G.I., construction hand, derrick rigger or what have you, not a man who had once had friends named Davos and Simpson, who had known a girl named Marcia and another girl named Sara;

a gay vivid girl and a quiet sober girl, and neither of them would ever be anything to him any more, except Sara, maybe, for a brief time, so that he could buy his freedom from Phil Stark.

He took a taxi to the Jungle Tavern. When he entered he saw that the stringed orchestra had been replaced by a seven-piece dance band. The place was jumping with its brassy music. The buxom blonde at the check room said brightly, "Back again, I see."

He gave her a crooked grin and entered the bar. The same bartender who had been on duty earlier served him a brandy and soda. He drank slowly, thinking in a kind of detached way that all of his life up until the last hour was gone now, all long ago and never to be lived again. He was someone different now, a stranger he didn't quite recognize, and didn't care to recognize. Even his face in the mirror behind the bar seemed changed, and he looked away quickly. He glanced nervously at his wrist watch. Eleven-fifty-five. She should be getting ready for her last appearance of the evening, he thought, and there was nothing to be gained by delaying what he had to do. Quick was the word. Do it as quickly and as painlessly as possible. And forget it. He gulped his drink and went back to her dressing room. No one stopped him.

He knocked on her door. Then he remembered that Blake Bowen had not knocked. He turned the knob and stepped inside. She was standing in the center of the small room and she turned quickly, her dark eyes wide with surprise. Her black hair was pinned in a thick knot on top of her small head. The stage make-up had been removed and her clear skin held a scrubbed shining look. All the spotlight glitter was gone and she was as Ramsey best remembered her from the last night in her apartment. The red silk robe was knotted loosely, revealing the beginnings of small round breasts.

Hastily she closed the robe. "Rack, you should knock. I—I am dressing."

"Bowen doesn't knock." He hadn't meant to say it. It was not part of his plan.

She ignored it. "You must not come here like this."

"Why not?" He closed the door and leaned against it. "I want to see you, Sara. What's wrong with that?"

89

She shook her head quickly. "No, no. You must not. Please."

He moved toward her. She retreated a few steps, holding the robe closely around her small slender body. "Listen, Sara," he said, "I want to talk to you . . ."

Behind him he heard the door open. Sara Colvin's breath caught in her throat. Ramsey turned. Blake Bowen stood there. Dim light from the hall glinted on his yellow hair and over the heavy shoulders beneath the midnight blue tuxedo. He smiled, but his eyes held an ugly light. They flicked contemptuously over Ramsey, and he said to the girl, "I told you to skip the last show. Why aren't you ready to leave?"

"I—I'll be ready in a few moments." She turned away, distressed, avoiding Ramsey's eyes, and sat at the dressing table. Her small pale hands fluttered over a row of jars and bottles and in the mirror Ramsey saw that her eyes were furtive and darting beneath the lowered black lashes.

Blake Bowen said, "Perhaps we'd better let her get dressed."

Ramsey turned. Bowen smiled and moved into the hall. Ramsey followed him slowly. As Bowen closed the door he smiled again and said, "Sara likes privacy—sometimes." The added word was like a slap in Ramsey's face.

They faced each other beneath the sickly glow from the overhead bulb. Bowen took a thin gold case from the inside pocket of his tuxedo, extracted a cigarette, delicately flicked flame from a gold lighter. His eyes above the flame were still and drowsy. "Bad night out," he said, drawing on the cigarette.

"Yes." Ramsey trusted himself to say the one word. He suddenly knew that he hated Blake Bowen, even more than he hated Phil Stark. He turned away.

"Goodbye," Bowen said.

Ramsey paused, half turned and said distinctly, "Good night."

Bowen's eyelids drooped a little. "Goodbye is what I meant. Stay away from here. I've told you before."

Ramsey gazed at him, feeling the hate. Then he turned away. He couldn't afford to have open trouble with Bowen, not before it was time for the trouble. And it wasn't time —not yet. He moved through the door at the end of the hall, feeling Bowen's eyes upon him.

He stood on the sidewalk and lit a cigarette. The brassy music came out to him. People were entering and leaving the Jungle Tavern. The sense of loneliness was almost a sickness. He had been lonely in the war, even with men all around him. In the last year he had met Pete Davos, and it hadn't been so bad after that. But now Pete was gone and Nevil Simpson seemed like someone he'd known long ago, in another life. Here in this city—in the world, really—there was only Sara Colvin. And he was planning to betray her—for five thousand dollars, to save his skin, to get him free of Phil Stark. He thought of Sara, of how it had been four months ago, before he'd met Marcia, before he'd gone to Mexico, and he thought of her as she must be now. Sara and Blake Bowen. Viciously he snapped his cigarette over the curb.

It was still raining and a cold wind blew off the gulf, making the rain slant and ripple along the street. He turned up the collar of his raincoat. A taxi drifted up, but he waved it away, and began to walk, keeping close to the walls and store fronts.

In ten minutes he came to the quiet side street and the small apartment building where Sara Colvin lived. The hedge and the dimly-lit foyer looked the same. Most of the lights in the building were out and the whole place held a quiet and peaceful air. He entered the foyer, saw that her name was still on one of the mail boxes. Feeling a sense of relief, he went back outside, glanced up and down the deserted street, and then moved to the shadows beyond the hedge, to the spot where he'd waited four months ago. He remembered suddenly and with a faint bitterness that he'd waited that night to apologize to her, to tell her that he was sorry for treating her as he had.

The thick trees along the boulevard partially sheltered him from the rain. He stood and watched the empty street and listened to the wind and the softly wet sounds of the moving branches above him. He didn't know how long he waited—twenty minutes, a half hour. At last a car turned in at the end of the street and stopped at the curb. He saw that it was a taxi and he stiffened. But an elderly couple got out and entered the apartment building. The street was quiet again.

The rain almost stopped and then began again, with more wind. He shivered a little. Then another car came down the street, a black Jaguar, with the top up. It stopped. A man and woman were inside and they seemed to be talking earnestly. The car's lights remained on and Ramsey heard the soft tick of the idling motor. Then the door opened and a woman got out. Ramsey saw instantly that it was Sara Colvin. The man leaned across the seat and said something to her in a low voice. "Yes, Blake," she replied and stepped back.

The Jaguar moved away, gathered speed, and disappeared around a corner with a red wink of tail lights. Sara Colvin walked quickly to the apartment entrance. She wore a loose coat, with a red scarf around her head. In the light from the foyer her small oval face looked pale and strained. She went inside and the door closed. Ramsey waited a moment and then followed her. The automatic elevator took him silently to the third floor. He moved down the hall to her door, hesitated a moment and then rapped softly.

He heard a movement inside, but the door remained closed. He rapped again, a trifle louder, and glanced quickly up and down the hall. It was empty and silent. A lock clicked then and the door opened a trifle. She gazed at him soberly.

"Please let me come in," he said quickly. "I want to talk to you."

"No, no, Rack. Please go away." She started to close the door, but he pushed it inward and stepped inside. She backed away from him, her eyes big. He closed the door and stood against it. Rain dripped from his hat and raincoat to the rug.

He removed the hat. "Sara, I had to see you. I'm going away, and—"

"Away?" she broke in. "When?"

"Tomorrow, maybe. I just wanted tó say goodbye, and to tell you again that I'm sorry."

Her eyes searched his face. "Sorry for what, Rack?"

Her grave steady gaze made him uneasy. "For everything," he said. "For going to Mexico without saying goodbye, and for . . ." He paused, not knowing how to go on.

"For that other girl?" she asked quietly. "Marcia Stockton, whose name is now Mrs. Carr, I believe?"

The thought of Marcia was like a stab wound. He looked at Sara quickly. Did she know that Marcia was dead? How could she know? Something stirred in his brain, and went away. There was nothing but sober intentness in Sara's eyes. "Yes," he said.

"I had no claim on you, but I—I think I hated her—then."

"You know her?" he was careful to put it in the present tense. "You mentioned her before."

"I know her by sight. She came to the club a few times, with the same man, and once with a large party. When I danced they threw money at me and laughed and one of the men tried to kiss me, and she took off her dress and danced. I—I was ashamed, and Blake was very angry. He made them all leave. But she is beautiful, Rack."

"Yes," he said, and wondered bleakly if that had been the night they had flown to Mexico, the night Marcia had married Jefferson Carr. All part of a merry evening, she had said, and he did not doubt that Sara's account of the drunken party was true. Rich and bored and restless, it was the kind of thing Marcia would do. As he gazed at Sara he thought that she looked very small and young in her plain white blouse, full red skirt and dainty high-heeled shoes. "Forget Marcia," he said. "Let Blake Bowen have her. I understand they are—friends."

Her eyes wavered for an instant, and then she looked at him half defiantly. "She means nothing to Blake. She—she pursued him, shamelessly, like she—"

"Like she pursued me?" he asked, feeling a faint coldness.

"I do not wish to talk about her." She turned away and added in a low voice, "Are you really going away?"

"Yes." He hesitated. Then: "I want you to come with me."

She turned to face him. "You do not mean that, Rack. It is just that you are lonely—we both are lonely. . . . Please go now."

"Why?"

"I—I cannot tell you, but it is best."

"Worried about Bowen?" As he spoke, the man's hard handsome face swam across his mind and it seemed that Bowen was leering at him. He shut out the picture quickly; there was no reason for it, and he must stick to a single purpose. He must make her believe that he was something he was not, convince her that he loved her truly, without

93

passion. What was the word Phil Stark had used? Platonic. He had to do it and he must not forget. "Is Bowen in love with you?" he asked.

"No, no. Nothing like that. Please do not ask me."

"What, then?" He took a step toward her.

There were sudden tears on her black lashes and her mouth trembled. "You should not be here, Rack. It is not —wise. But I am glad. All of the time you were away I thought of you, even though I was certain I would never see you again. And when you came to my dressing room tonight, I—I cannot tell you how happy I was."

"You didn't act very happy."

"My aunt in Mazatlan, she taught me never to be bold." She lowered her gaze. "Perhaps, if I had forgotten my aunt's teachings when we first met, you would not have gone to—to her."

"Marcia?" It was difficult for him to say the name.

She nodded.

"Did it matter so much to you?"

She looked up at him. "It mattered very much," she said gravely. "So much it—it frightened me. When Pete told me, I—I do not know what I felt."

"You hated her," he said bleakly. "You said you hated her."

"It was wrong of me, but I could not help it."

He thought, *Because of me, or because of Blake Bowen? But you can stop hating her now, honey, whatever the reason. Marcia is beyond hate and love, especially her kind of love, and it is not for her now, never no more. No more martinis on the terrace, no rides in the moonlight, no drunken flights to Mexico, no dancing with her clothes off in a public tavern, no more sweet, wild ecstasy . . .*

"You came out of nowhere," Sara Colvin said, a soft shine in her dark eyes. "Rackwell Ramsey, such an odd name, a lovely name. Then you went away. Now you have returned—for a short time, perhaps, but you are here now, and I am glad."

He gazed at her in surprise, and he felt the uneasiness again. "I thought you wanted me to go?"

A shadow crossed her eyes, and then she smiled. "If you are going away tomorrow, I will not worry tonight. . . . Rack, your coat is wet. Please remove it."

94

He was puzzled, but he took off the raincoat, laid it on the floor along the wall and placed his hat on top of it.

"But let me hang them up," she protested.

He smiled at her. "Don't bother."

She said, almost shyly, "Would you like a drink?"

"Yes—if you'll have one, too."

"Of course." There was now a dancing light in her eyes, and a strange excitement he had never seen before. "Scotch, Rack? I have some Scotch."

"With water," he said, wondering bleakly if Blake Bowen liked Scotch, too.

She whirled away, smiling at him over a shoulder, and entered the small kitchen.

He moved to a chair and sat down with a sigh. He was tired and his head still ached dully, but the familiar little apartment had a soothing effect upon him. In a strange way it was a little like coming home, and he remembered the last time he'd sat in the same chair, holding Sara. It came back to him vividly, that last night, before he'd met Marcia. He stirred uneasily. The thought of what he had to do was like a devil's fork prodding his brain.

She came into the room with two tall glasses. He took one, and she sat in a chair opposite him. He could hear the rain on the windows and for the moment he felt safe, protected from the world. Then he thought immediately of Blake Bowen, and took a long swallow of the Scotch.

"Why are you so quiet, Rack?"

He smiled. "Just tired, I guess."

"Where are you going? Is it far?"

He thought quickly. "I have the promise of a job in Wyoming."

Her eyes clouded. "That is very far, is it not?"

"Pretty far." He drank again.

"Will you write to me?"

"I'm not much good at writing letters." He paused. "Sara, I meant what I said. Come with me."

"I cannot, even if you truly wanted me." She looked down at her glass, and he saw the faint flush on her cheeks. "I—I want to tell you something, before you go away."

He waited, watching her.

She looked up. Her eyes were level and direct. "Rack, there comes a time when a person must begin to live their

95

own life, for better or for worse. One cannot be tied forever to childhood teachings."

He was oddly embarrassed, yet happy and faintly exultant. It should be easy now, if he played his cards carefully. He remembered his days in Vegas and Reno; it was like being dealt an ace before he'd had a look at his hole card. He leaned forward and touched her cheek. It was hot. Her lashes were wet and he felt her tremble. Gently he took the glass from her fingers, placed it with his on a low table, and pulled her to her feet. She came against him with a little sigh and her lips were warm and clinging. He sensed an abandonment in her that he had not dreamed existed, and his hands moved over her small slim body.

"Rack," she whispered against his lips, "I am not afraid any more, not with you."

"Sara, listen—"

The telephone began to ring, a shrill and piercing sound in the quiet room. Ramsey stiffened, but he held her close and said, "Let it ring."

She moved within his arms. "No, I must answer."

He held her tighter. The phone rang again.

"Rack—please." Her voice was desperate, and she struggled. "If I do not answer, he will— Please let me go."

He released her. She ran to the phone, picked it up and said breathlessly, "Yes?"

Ramsey heard the metallic sound of a male voice. He watched Sara's strained face. "Yes," she said again. "I was in bed. . . . No, of course not. . . . Yes, I will—tomorrow morning. . . . Yes, yes. . . . Good night." She replaced the phone and turned slowly.

"Bowen?" he asked.

She nodded. "He—he wanted to tell me about some changes in the act for tomorrow night."

"At two o'clock in the morning?"

She nodded again, her eyes wavering. "That—that is when he works—at night."

He decided to try and bring it out in the open, at least part of it, if he could. "What is Bowen to you?"

She twisted her fingers together nervously. "Nothing, Rack. I told you. He is merely my employer. Please believe me." Her eyes were imploring.

He made an impatient bitter gesture and moved to the door.

96

"Do not go, Rack."

"Why not?" he asked coldly.

"Because I—I want you to stay."

He stood by the door, watching her. He was botching it he thought. The damned phone call had mixed him up, thrown him off balance. But instinct told him that maybe it had been a good thing. He moved to her, placed his hands on her shoulders. "Sara, let's get out of this. Go with me to Wyoming."

She closed her eyes and began to cry silently. "I—I want to, Rack. I want to leave this city. But I cannot . . ."

His hands tightened on her shoulders. "Tell me why you can't."

She lowered her head and didn't answer.

He dropped his hands and stepped back. "Good night, Sara."

She looked up. Her cheeks were wet. "Will I see you before you go away?"

"Maybe," he said shortly, trying not to see the hurt and bewilderment in her eyes. He knew he could stay; she had asked him to stay. But this was not the time, not after the phone call, and he no longer had any real desire. His head ached and his body felt drained and numb. It had been a long day. Much had happened, and more was still to happen. He had made some progress, a Judas progress, but maybe she deserved to have one Judas in her life. If she had only one, she would be lucky.

She watched him silently as he picked up his hat and raincoat. He smiled at her as he went out. As he closed the door he knew he would remember the look in her eyes for a long time. As he went down in the elevator, he thought bitterly, *Act One*.

CHAPTER 14

THE RAIN still came down, drenching the city, the wind blowing it against the buildings. Ramsey walked to the corner and looked for a taxi, but the long wide street was empty, with only the lights of a few bars and all-night restaurants glinting in the wetness. It took him twenty minutes of fast walking to reach the Gulf Hotel. He went to bed, but it was a long time before he slept restlessly.

He came awake slowly. The bright ceiling light was shining in his eyes. He sat up, drugged with sleep. Two persons stood at the foot of the bed, both of them smiling at him in friendly fashion. One was an over-dressed kid with a thick loop of chestnut hair falling over his pale forehead. The other was a thin brown man in a tan snap-brim hat and a tight, dark blue, pin-striped suit. Rain spotted the brown man's hat and glinted in the kid's hair.

The brown man said, "We're sorry to disturb your slumber." A gold tooth winked as he spoke.

"Yeah." The kid grinned vacantly.

Ramsey found his voice. "That door was locked."

"Locks," the brown man said. "Hah!" He turned to the kid and said sadly, "He was all nice and comfy and we disturbed him."

The kid giggled and pulled the back of a hand over a loose wet mouth. Ramsey saw that he was quite drunk.

"How about getting the hell out of here?" Ramsey said. "You've got the wrong room."

The brown man smiled at him tenderly and then spoke to the kid. "The light, Sonny, the light."

"Yeah." The kid reached a wavering hand for the wall switch.

Ramsey gathered his legs beneath him and leaped for the thin brown man. But he was far too slow. The light went out and in the same instant something solid slammed against his head. He hit the floor on his right shoulder, tangled in the bed sheets. The dark room seemed to be whirling with purple-bursting stars. He tried to squirm out of the sheets, but his movements were slow and fumbling. From above him he heard the kid's liquid giggle, and a quick intake of breath. He knew what was coming and he covered his head with his hands. A blunt object thudded down between his fingers. A great flower of pain blossomed behind his eyes, and the blackness came speeding at him . . .

Cold water hit his face with stinging force. Faint light from the window cast a dull glow over the room, and through a watery haze he saw the kid standing unsteadily over him holding a pitcher in one hand, a glass in the other. He made an underhanded throwing motion with the glass, and Ramsey moved his head instinctively. The water splashed down behind his ears. The kid giggled. Ramsey reached an arm for the bed, tried to pull himself up. He had one raging thought; get his hands on the kid. A shadow crossed his vision and a foot appeared before his eyes, a foot in a two-toned brown shoe with a very sharp toe. He twisted his head, trying to avoid the shoe, but the toe struck his chin sharply. Ramsey hit the floor and clawed at the rug.

From the darkness above him the brown man said, "Stay away from Sara Colvin, and stay away from the Jungle Tavern. That's all, brother."

Ramsey moved his legs feebly. And then he didn't move at all for a while. The blackjack thudded down once more and he almost welcomed the rushing blackness. It was as if a sweet anesthetic was wafting him off to peaceful sleep. He heard the kid's idiotic laughter and a door slammed. The brief silence merged into one big silence, and the last thing he remembered was the prickly feel of the rug against his cheek.

He shivered and rolled over on his back. In the gloom he could see the curtains billowing inward from the window. A cold breeze and a faint mist of rain hit his face. It felt good, but still he shivered. His head pounded wickedly and there was a dry fuzzy taste in his mouth. Grunting, he pushed himself to a sitting position, pulled up his knees and hugged them, trying to stop the shivering. He was sweating, and yet he was cold.

Something moved by the window. Ramsey raised his head, peered intently. There was a remembered odor of burning pipe tobacco. A soft voice said reproachfully, "Kind of a bad beginning, son."

Ramsey saw him then. The huge bulk moved away from the window and light from the street fell over the brown tweed coat. "So it's you," Ramsey said bitterly. With the shivering, it was hard to control his voice. "You were a big help. Thank you very much."

"Listen," the fat man named Victor said gently, "I'm supposed to follow you, and that's all. If you get into trouble, you're on your own. Remember what Phil told you."

"Stark." Ramsey said the word like a curse. "You go back and tell him to go to hell. I'm through."

He heard the fat man sigh heavily. "You don't mean that. Right now the police are looking for the person who murdered Mrs. Carr." He paused and sighed again. "Remember—Phil is holding positive evidence identifying you as the killer."

"Go away," Ramsey groaned.

Victor lumbered slowly to the door and opened it. "Blake Bowen's boys will be watching you from now on. Be careful." He opened the door wide and his fat body loomed against the light from the hall. "Uh—Phil told me to give you a message, if I had a chance."

"What?"

"He said to tell Romeo that faint heart never won fair lady."

Ramsey said a word, a short one.

"I just do what Phil tells me," Victor said. The door closed softly.

Slowly Ramsey pushed himself to his feet, walked unsteadily into the bath room and soaked his head in cold water. It helped a little. He dried his head with a towel and looked in the mirror. There was a small swollen bruised spot on his chin where the brown man had kicked him, and the top of his head was very tender, with a slight lumpiness. He returned to the bedroom, closed the window and inspected the door. The lock was sprung, the wood beside it splintered. He propped a chair beneath the knob and got back into bed.

The room was filled with the gray dawn before he slept. He dreamed that he was back in the army with Pete Davos, crouched behind a crumbling church. Machine gun bullets were chipping the wall above them, and red hell was breaking loose on the road beyond. Planes snarled above them and shrapnel shattered against the sky in lovely starry patterns. Pete grinned at him. His face was bearded and sweaty, and his helmet strap was loose. In his dream Ramsey returned Pete's grin, and he was happy.

It was almost noon when he wakened. He lay still, staring at the ceiling, while the remembrance of the night and

100

the day before crept across his brain. He closed his eyes, remembering all of it. After a while he got stiffly out of bed. As he peered into the bath room mirror he thought with surprise that he didn't look bad at all. The lumps on his head couldn't be seen, and the swelling on his chin had gone down. He shaved, showered, dressed and went down to the restaurant. There was no room service at the Gulf Hotel. After he'd eaten, he returned to the room, sat by the open window and smoked a cigarette. The rain had stopped, but a mist seemed to hang over the city. A damp breeze blew in from the Gulf. He looked at his watch. Eleven-thirty in the morning.

The phone rang, startling him. He went to it, hesitated, and then picked it up. "Hello."

"Rack, are you—all right?" It was Sara Colvin. Her voice sounded strained and queer.

"Yes," he said. "Why?"

"I—I was worried about you."

He gripped the phone tighter. "Why?" he asked again.

"Rack, I—I am frightened. Will you come and get me? I know it is a lot to ask, but I have no one else . . ."

"What's the matter?" he asked sharply.

She spoke swiftly. "I should have told you last night. I cannot talk now. Will you come? Now?"

"Yes."

"Oh, thank you, Rack! I will wait for you. Please, please hurry." The receiver clicked in his ear.

He put on his hat and raincoat and went out. Down in the lobby he saw the fat man named Victor leaning against the cigar counter. He peered at Ramsey over the top of a newspaper. As Ramsey went past, he snarled, "Don't you ever sleep?"

Victor folded the paper and followed Ramsey to the street. A taxi pulled up and as Ramsey started to get in, Victor said, "Where are you going?"

"Come along and find out."

Victor hesitated, glancing worriedly up and down the street.

"Get in, get in," Ramsey said impatiently. "I'm in a hurry."

Victor shook his head and backed away.

Ramsey slammed the taxi door, and gave the driver Sara Colvin's address. As they drove away, he looked back

101

through the rear window. He saw Victor get into the blue-and-gray Ford station wagon and follow them, keeping a half block behind. When the taxi stopped at Sara Colvin's apartment, the Ford nosed into a parking space three cars behind. Ramsey told the taxi driver to wait and got out. As he did so, a new black Dodge sedan pulled away from the opposite side of the street, moving swiftly. As it passed, Ramsey had a fleeting glimpse of three persons in the front seat, and with a sickening shock he recognized his two visitors of the night before—the thin brown man and the kid with the chestnut hair. Sara Colvin was huddled between them. She saw Ramsey on the sidewalk, and she began to struggle, her eyes big and scared in her small pale face. As Ramsey stood frozen, he saw the kid's arm go around Sara and pull her down in the seat. Then the Dodge was past, roaring for the corner.

Ramsey stood still, sweating with indecision. He was too late, he thought. She was in trouble and had asked him to help her, because she had no one else. He could guess the trouble now, and he knew that he had caused it. So what? Maybe she deserved to be in trouble. He was in plenty of trouble himself. And then he remembered that it was only through Sara that he could get out of his own trouble. He walked back to the station wagon, aware that it was raining again, and leaned in the window.

"Come in out of the rain," Victor invited, puffing on his pipe.

"Did you see them?"

Victor nodded. "Sure. Sonny and Rafael. Full names Thomas Kingseed and Rafael Mendez. Blake Bowen's hired men and bad ones, too." He avoided Ramsey's gaze. "They—uh—had the girl with them."

"She called me," Ramsey said. "Asked me to help her. But I was too late. They got her. What am I supposed to do now?"

Victor turned his head. "That's up to you," he said soberly. "It looks to me like you got Bowen worried and he's putting the girl under wraps. . . . You're getting wet, son."

A car with a long radio antenna and with the word *Police* emblazoned on its side cruised slowly along the street. One of the two officers in the front seat glanced curiously at Ramsey standing beside the station wagon, and

102

Ramsey had a sudden strange feeling of fear. He averted his face, involuntarily. The policeman's gaze flicked over him, and the cruiser kept going.

Victor said in an unsteady voice, "I sure wouldn't want the cops to nab you while you was talking to me." He puffed nervously on his pipe. "I don't know what you got in mind, but you can't quit."

Ramsey knew that Victor was right. He was in too deeply now, and Phil Stark would never let him quit. He had a sudden and frantic impulse to run. What if he pulled out now, headed south over the Border, back to Tampico and Nevil Simpson. How far would he get? To the city limits, maybe?

Victor said gently, "Don't get any ideas. You can't run away from trouble."

"I can try," Ramsey said in a tight voice.

Victor shook his head slowly. "Don't. It would mean my job if you skipped."

"That would be too damn bad," Ramsey sneered.

Victor sighed. "I know how you feel, but look at it from my side. I work for Phil Stark. I got a wife and three kids, and he pays pretty good. It's better than walking a mail route, like I used to do. I do what Phil wants, and I don't ask no questions. He plays square—I know his tables and wheels are straight. As long as he don't double-cross or cheat anybody I'll play square with him, and I can sleep at night."

He paused, puffed thoughtfully on the pipe. "I'm telling you this because I want you to know I got nothing against you. It's just my job to see that you don't leave town." He sighed again and gazed at the pipe. "I ain't had any sleep since the night before last, but that's my job. The sooner you do what Phil wants the sooner I can go home and see my family and get some sleep."

"It's a dirty frame, and you know it," Ramsey said, trying not to think of Sara Colvin's pale frightened face as she sat in the car between Rafael and Sonny.

"It's a square deal," Victor said stubbornly, "according to the way Phil looks at things. You killed Mrs. Carr, but he's willing to overlook that if you'll get him Blake Bowen's money. Dope money. To me, that's like finding it. It don't belong to nobody, except maybe the poor devils who bought the dope. If Phil can get it, good for him. What you have to do to get it is no concern of his. You already got murder on your conscience. And don't forget—if Phil says he'll turn you over to the cops, he'll do it, if you don't play along. I don't know what you're going to do now, but you better do something." He peered at Ramsey gravely. "Phil ain't unreasonable, but when he wants a job done—well, he wants it done."

Ramsey said, "What happened at Jeff Carr's house last night?"

Victor's eyes shifted. "Now, there's no sense in dragging out dead cats," he said reproachfully. "I followed you from Phil's place to the house and waited outside. I heard the shot and ran in, like I told you. There you was, on the floor, with the gun in your hand, and Mrs. Carr was dead."

"You didn't see anybody?"

"Nobody but you."

"Damn it—how could I have shot her, when I was knocked cold? That gun was planted in my hand."

Victor shrugged. "I only know what I saw."

"To hell with you, Victor."

"All right," the fat man said soberly, "if that's the way you feel. Sticks and stones can break my bones, but words—"

"Have you got a gun?" Ramsey said.

"Yes, but you can't have it."

"Will you drive me to the Jungle Tavern?"

Victor moved uncomfortably. "I can't do that. Bowen or one of his boys might see me. Phil wouldn't like that."

"And neither would you."

"No," Victor admitted, "I wouldn't. Blake Bowen is, well, tough, and he don't fool around with people who mess into his business."

"You've got to think of the wife and kids," Ramsey sneered. He pulled his head out of the car window.

"That's right," Victor agreed. "Good luck."

Ramsey walked away from him.

"Hey," Victor called. "Wait. I almost forgot."

Ramsey turned and went back. The thought of Sara was a nagging worry. He didn't know what he was going to do about her—he only knew that he had to do something. He stopped at the station wagon and gazed coldly at the fat man.

"Maybe you'd better read this." Victor handed him a folded newspaper.

Ramsey leaned inside the car, opened the paper. The murder of Marcia Carr was on the front page, with a carry-over to page two, where there were pictures, one of Marcia in a bathing suit. He gazed at her laughing face, at her tall slender figure, and grimly his eyes dropped to the text. He scanned the headlines and skipped through the story:

OIL HEIRESS MURDERED. . . . Mrs. Jefferson Carr Found Shot to Death. . . . Police Comb City for Mystery Killer. . . . Taxi Driver Says He Can Identify Night Visitor. . . . Murdered woman wife of prominent attorney. . . . Mysterious phone call summons police immediately after shooting. . . . Robbery not motive. . . . Husband, away on business trip to Austin, told by police of tragedy. . . . Victim daughter of the late Clinton Stockton, southern Texas multi-millionaire oil man. . . All Border stations have been alerted. . . . State police and sheriff's departments have established road blocks. . . . An arrest is expected momentarily. . . .

Ramsey stopped reading and looked at Victor.

"Read the box." The fat man pointed with his pipe stem.

Ramsey's gaze returned to the paper. Halfway down the front page was a boxed item in eight-point black-face type with a fourteen-point head: *LATE FLASH—Police have requested all citizens to watch for a man about thirty years old, weighing about one hundred and ninety pounds, six feet tall, and wearing when last seen a light tan raincoat and a dark brown hat. He is wanted for questioning in connection with the murder of Mrs. Jefferson Carr. The description was given the police by George Hanover, 46, a driver for the Suburban Cab Company, who says he picked up the man at a gasoline station on the gulf road across from the Starlight Club and drove him to the Carr residence shortly before Mrs. Carr was murdered. Any information regarding this man should be given the police immediately.*

Ramsey handed the paper back to Victor. "Thanks. Do you have a false mustache and a putty nose I could borrow?"

"The cops don't have much to go on—so far," Victor said. He gazed out at the street and added, "Phil Stark could give them your name and a complete description."

Ramsey said harshly, "And so could Blake Bowen and

105

Sara Colvin and Jefferson Carr, and so could you. But I didn't kill her."

Victor continued to gaze at the street. He looked tired and his eyes were red-rimmed. Ramsey turned angrily and walked swiftly away. At the corner he signaled a cruising taxi, got in, and told the driver to take him to the Jungle Tavern.

"It ain't open yet," the driver said.

"I know it," Ramsey snapped. "Hurry." As the taxi pulled away, he looked back. The Ford station wagon was right behind them. He could see Victor behind the wheel and the stubborn tilt of the pipe in his mouth. He leaned back in the seat, knowing that he was scared. But he had to find Sara and get her away from those two men. What were their names? Sonny and Rafael, Victor had said. Blake Bowen's boys. When he thought of Sonny, he forgot his fright and felt the rage again. But he must think only of Sara, he told himself, and Phil Stark, and maybe Blake Bowen, and of what he had to do to gain his freedom. He must think of that, and not about how Sara had struggled in the car when she'd seen him on the sidewalk at her apartment. He must forget the scared imploring look of her, and that in her fear she had turned to him, because she had no one else to turn to.

And how had Marcia know that he was in town . . . ?

Up ahead he saw the marquee of the Jungle Tavern. He leaned forward and told the driver to stop a block beyond. The driver nodded, and Ramsey sat tensely on the edge of the seat. Maybe she would be there and maybe she wouldn't, he thought. But he had to find her, and it was a place to start. After that, he'd try Blake Bowen's house or apartment, or wherever he lived.

They passed the Jungle Tavern and at the next intersection the taxi stopped. Ramsey got out, paid the driver before the traffic light changed, and walked back, hurrying in the fine mist of rain. In the daylight the small court behind the night club looked different, tawdry, with garbage cans arrayed against a wall. Beyond the rear door and around a sort of L there was a parking and unloading area littered with waste paper. A new black Dodge sedan was nosed up against a small loading dock. Ramsey stopped and took a deep breath. So she was here.

He walked swiftly to the car, and peered inside. The

106

key was in the ignition lock. He took it out, dropped it into his raincoat pocket, went up some wooden steps to the dock and tried the knob of a door. To his surprise, the door wasn't locked. He hesitated a moment, his heart pounding, and wished he had a gun. Slowly he pushed the door inward, thinking that Sonny and Rafael had really been in a hurry, and he paused again. It was very quiet. The sound of the traffic in the street seemed far away, and he felt again the deadly loneliness. He pushed the door a little more. Maybe they're waiting for me inside, he thought, and he swallowed. Through the partially open door he saw the end of a huge stove and a row of pots and pans on steel hooks. There was no sound, no movement, nothing. He knew that the place did not open until four in the afternoon, but he wondered if any of the help would be working at this time of day. He waited another instant, and then ducked quickly inside, closed the door silently and stood against it.

The big kitchen was silent and empty. He moved slowly across it to a swinging door, opened it a crack and peered through. He could see the edge of the dance floor, an expanse of tables, and the bar through the alcove at the far end of the big room. The place was as empty and as still as only a night club can be at noon. He left the kitchen and paused, listening. From beyond the bar, probably from the hall leading to Sara's dressing room, he heard faint voices. A door slammed. Then silence. He tip-toed between the tables to the bar, saw that the door to the hall was open. He peered cautiously. Sara's dressing room door was open, too. The two doors beyond it were closed. The ceiling bulb burned dimly.

He took four slow steps forward. And he stopped. There was a thudding sound, as though a chair had fallen over, and then a man's voice, harsh, but incoherent, and another sound, a woman sobbing. Ramsey waited, trying to decide from behind which of the two closed doors the sounds were coming from. Then the sobbing stopped and the silence came down like settling dust. There was a soft furtive movement behind him. He sensed it more than he heard it, and he whirled.

The kid with the chestnut hair was standing just inside the doorway leading to the bar. In his right hand he held a black automatic pistol. In his left was an open whisky

107

bottle with a bright label. His thick hair fell over his narrow pale forehead. His eyes were hot and glassy and he stood there swaying happily, his loose wet mouth open, grinning like an idiot.

Ramsey stood still, his gaze on the gun. The kid held it loosely, carelessly, as if he didn't know he held it. He moved forward, stepping lightly, lifting his feet high, like a cat walking on fly paper. He mumbled something that made no sense. When he was three feet away he stopped, swayed, giggled shrilly, and slowly raised the gun. He held it at arm's length, like a shooter on a range, aiming at Ramsey's chest, and he squinted one eye down the wavering muzzle.

CHAPTER 15

RAMSEY DROPPED to a crouch, leaped forward, came up under the gun and grabbed the kid's arm. Holding the arm, he jerked the kid forward and slammed a fist against the kid's chin. The kid's head snapped back and his body went limp. Ramsey caught him on his shoulder before he hit the floor. The bottle bounded over the floor spouting whisky. It hit the wall and settled down to a steady amber gurgle. Ramsey stumbled a little beneath the kid's weight. He heard a faint thud, saw that the kid had dropped the gun. He stopped, picked up the gun, and went off balance. As he staggered forward, he felt a sudden hot pain in his side, just above his belt. He flung the kid from his shoulder and stood panting. The kid rolled over and slumped against the wall, his hair in his eyes, the bright gleam of a knife in his hand.

Ramsey felt his side. No blood yet, but it burned. He looked at the two closed doors. They remained closed, and the man's voice was shouting something; perhaps his shouting had drowned out the noise the bouncing bottle had made, Ramsey thought, and the sounds of the scuffle with the kid.

"Fooled you, didn't I?" the kid said softly. "I hate guns,

108

but Blake gave it to me. I like knives." He pushed himself to his feet and leaned unsteadily against the wall, holding the knife.

Ramsey watched him, wondering if he should hit him with the gun.

"Come on," the kid whispered. He high-stepped toward Ramsey, holding the knife out in front.

"Stay away," Ramsey muttered, glancing at the closed doors.

The kid lurched forward. Ramsey side-stepped and watched him, holding the gun. The kid turned, giggling, his mouth wet, and once more he sprang with the knife. Ramsey lifted a foot and kicked him in the stomach. The kid doubled over, gasping. Ramsey stepped in and swung the automatic against the kid's head. The kid shuddered, but he didn't go down. He turned toward Ramsey, crouching, his legs wobbling. There was blood on his temple where the gun had hit him, and a dreamy light in his eyes. He lurched forward and the knife snaked out. Once more Ramsey side-stepped and swung the gun. The kid went to his knees, his eyes tightly closed. Then he shook his head, raised a bloody face to Ramsey, and hobbled forward on his knees, jabbing with the knife.

Ramsey felt a little sick, like a man trying to kill a snake that wouldn't die. He hit the kid once more, not with the gun, but with his fist, and he put his shoulder and arm into it. The kid expelled a long sigh and pitched forward to the floor.

Ramsey leaned against the wall and sucked air into his lungs. His side burned from the knife wound and he felt the warm dampness of blood, but he paid no attention. He watched the two closed doors, and he heard muffled voices. He hefted the gun, a Colt .38, checked the clip, saw that it was full, with a cartridge in the firing chamber. Then he edged slowly along the wall until he came to Sara's dressing room. It was empty. He moved on to the first closed door beyond. The voices behind it grew louder. Ramsey flattened himself against the wall. The knob turned and the door opened.

The thin brown man backed out. There was sweat on his face and he looked worried. He was lifting his hands in a placating gesture. "All right, *all right*. Don't you worry,

109

Boss. I'll take care of it, real good. Me and Sonny will find him. He can't get—"

Ramsey raised the gun and chopped down. The brown man crumpled without a sound. Ramsey leaped over him into the room, the gun out in front. He was in an office, elegantly furnished. Thick tan rug, embossed wall paper, soft indirect lighting, a huge polished desk, filing cabinets, deep chairs covered with bright damask. He didn't actually see it all, but he was aware of it. Blake Bowen stood facing him, his heavy handsome face blank with surprise. Sara Colvin was in a chair behind him. Her eyes were big with fear and pain, and there was a thin trickle of blood on her chin. When she saw Ramsey her eyes grew bigger and her lips moved, but he couldn't hear any words.

For a second there was complete silence. Then Bowen's gaze moved from Ramsey to the silent form of the brown man lying in the doorway. "Rafael," he said harshly, "get up."

"He can't," Ramsey said.

Bowen ignored him. "Sonny!" he bawled at the doorway. "Where are you?"

"Shut up," Ramsey snapped. He pointed the gun at a chair against the wall. "Sit down."

Bowen's gaze swung to Ramsey. The surprise was gone and his eyes showed nothing but contempt and an ugly mounting rage. "I made a mistake," he said from between his teeth. "I should have told Sonny and Rafael to do a complete job on you last night."

"Sit down," Ramsey said, moving the gun. "I told you before."

Bowen spat two words, one of them obscene.

Ramsey swung the gun. The sight on the muzzle ripped an inch gash in Bowen's chin. Sara Colvin cried out faintly, a kind of whimpering bird sound, as Bowen lunged for Ramsey. Ramsey stopped him with a kick in the stomach. Bowen gagged and swung away, his head down. He vomited on the soft tan rug. Ramsey watched him with a strange detachment. Bowen stood bent over, one hand fumbling for a handkerchief in the breast pocket of a sky-blue cashmere jacket. He held the handkerchief to his mouth and turned. His face was congested and his eyes were watery from the vomiting.

110

Ramsey said, "Stand aside. I'm leaving now. Sara goes with me."

Bowen wiped his mouth, tossed the handkerchief into a leather waste basket, took a deep shuddering breath and stood up straight. He swallowed several times. The black rage was still in his eyes, but he spoke in a surprisingly quiet voice. "Who are you?"

"Ramsey's the name."

"I know that." Bowen swallowed again and felt his throat. "Who are you working for?"

"Myself." Ramsey backed to the door. "Come on, Sara."

She got to her feet slowly. Bowen spoke sharply, without taking his gaze from Ramsey. "Sit down, Sara."

She remained standing, watching Ramsey. Her dress was torn at the neckline, revealing a smooth white shoulder. Ramsey said to Bowen, "Don't try to stop us."

Bowen smiled, but there was hate in his eyes. "Government man, perhaps?" he said to Ramsey. "Treasury Department? You want Miss Colvin for a—a witness? Is that it? I'm sure we can reach an agreement. How much?"

Ramsey held out an arm and Sara Colvin came against him. He held her with his left arm and leveled the gun at Bowen. They backed toward the door.

Bowen mouthed something incoherent and lunged for them. Ramsey aimed at Bowen's left leg and pulled the trigger. The walls seemed to rock with the blasting sound. Bowen fell to his knees in an attitude of prayer, but he struggled forward, his face contorted. His left leg was like the stump of a leg. It trailed behind him as he crawled. "Sonny!" he cried. "Rafael!"

Ramsey stepped forward and hit him with the gun. Bowen went down and he didn't move. Blood from his leg began to stain the tan rug. Ramsey leaned over him and felt for a gun. He didn't find one and he wasn't surprised. If he'd had a gun, he would have used it before now. Ramsey went to Sara Colvin. "Are you all right?"

She nodded dumbly, her eyes a little wild, her fingers plucking at the torn dress in an attempt to cover her bare shoulder.

"Go to the kitchen," he told her. "Wait for me. We'll have to hurry." He turned her around, helped her over the still form of Rafael, and gave her a slight push down the hall. She looked at the kid named Sonny lying against the wall, but she didn't speak and kept going. "Two minutes," Ramsey called after her.

She made no sign that she had heard him, and disappeared through the doorway at the end of the hall. He began to sweat. It was a stupid thing to do, he thought. Now that he had found her, he shouldn't let her out of sight, not even for two minutes. He'd had a hazy notion of finding some rope, twine, something, with which to tie Bowen, Rafael and Sonny, to delay their inevitable pursuit, but it was silly. Bowen wouldn't be chasing anyone, not with a bullet in his leg, but Rafael and Sonny wouldn't be delayed long. There was no help for that, unless he shot them. He gazed at the forms of the two men. Rafael was breathing heavily but still unconscious. Sonny was stirring a little. Ramsey made up his mind and moved swiftly down the hall.

She was waiting for him in the kitchen, standing by the door. He felt a sudden relief and smiled at her. She gazed at him silently, with something like hysteria in her eyes. He took her arm and said, "Take it easy," and led her out to the Dodge parked by the loading platform. As they drove out he glanced back and saw that the court was still empty. When he was out on the street and cruising in the heavy traffic he took the gun from his coat pocket and laid it on the seat beside his leg.

Sara Colvin said in a shaky voice, "Thank you, Rack. That was a—a brave thing to do."

He didn't answer and kept his gaze ahead, his hands gripping the wheel. He was not brave, he thought bleakly—just scared and cornered. Even a rat will fight when he's cornered, even a mouse or a mewling kitten.

She spoke with a faint shrillness. "He—he slapped me, Rack. Blake did. Rafael watched and laughed. Sonny was supposed to be outside watching. Blake said things to me, bad things, about you and me. He—he was like a crazy man. He—"

"Never mind," he said harshly. "It's all right now. Forget it."

He felt her hand on his arm. "Thank you, Rack."

He shot her a glance. She was watching him intently, her eyes big and dark in her pale face. The blood on her chin was drying. She looks like hell, he thought. Like a ravaged angel.

She said gravely, "Rack, I must tell you this: Blake hates you and perhaps he fears you, because of me. He knew you were with me last night. That is why he telephoned me. Then he sent Rafael and Sonny to the apartment. When you left, they followed you to your hotel. Blake told me today that I would never see you again. Did—did they hurt you?"

"No." He kept his gaze straight ahead.

"I am glad," she said in her soft voice. "Blake telephoned me again this morning. He was angry because I was with you last night, against his orders. He said he was going to punish me, that I was to stay with him now, to live with him, because he did not trust me. He told me to pack my clothes, that Sonny and Rafael were coming to get me. That is when I called you . . ."

He said, "I've asked you before—what is Blake Bowen to you?"

Her eyes wavered and her small body seemed to shrink. "I will tell you, Rack. But please give me a little time. . . . Where are we going?"

He didn't answer. He had no answer for her yet. Not until she told him about the money in the safe deposit box. He held the wheel tightly, watching the traffic ahead. The knife wound in his side was burning and beginning to feel stiff. He glanced at the gas gauge. Half full. He looked in the rear-view mirror. A blue and gray Ford station wagon was cruising along three cars behind them. Victor was still on his tail, but keeping a safe distance. He wondered if Sonny and Rafael were on the prowl for him yet. He increased his speed a little. At the next intersection he stopped for a red light, and while he waited for the green signal he made up his mind.

He looked sideways at Sara Colvin. She sat quietly, staring straight ahead with dark haunted eyes. She had wiped the blood from her chin, but her lower lip was slightly swollen and bruised-looking. The torn dress drooped down from her bare shoulder. He reached out and touched her arm. She looked at him quickly. He smiled. "I didn't answer you back there because I was thinking." The light turned green and as he prodded the Dodge ahead, he said, "You don't want to go back to Bowen and the Jungle Tavern?"

113

"No, no—I cannot. Never will I go back there." In her fear and emotion the faint accent was stronger.

"All right," he said. "That's what I wanted to know. Don't talk any more now." He watched for a certain street and when he came to it, he turned right and fed gas. After a few blocks he came to another red light and stopped. Once more he looked in the rear-view mirror. The station wagon was still behind him, two cars away now. Victor was getting reckless, he thought grimly. A tall policeman stood on the sidewalk beside them, gazing absently up and down the street. His gaze flicked over Ramsey and Sara and passed on. The light changed and Ramsey crossed the intersection at a normal speed, not wanting to attract the attention of the policeman, or of anyone, but he fought an impulse to hurry, to get far away from something he couldn't see, but which he knew was close, or would be close very soon. Victor didn't count. He wasn't worried about the fat man in the pay of Phil Stark, but there was the law, and Blake Bowen's henchmen. And he thought with a kind of sadness that there was no time for any decent build-up with Sara, no time for even a pretense of finesse. That time was gone. He should have pushed things the night before. That had been the time, but Bowen's phone call had messed it up . . .

The traffic thinned as they approached the fringes of the city. He increased his speed and at last he came to the gulf road. He swung onto it, pushed the car to sixty and held it there. The city limits sign flashed past and he fed more gas. Seventy, seventy-five. Off to the right the gulf rolled like oil in the mist and the overcast. He kept his eyes on the road, but he was aware that Sara Colvin sat quietly beside him, asking no questions, trusting him.

The lane rushed toward him and he braked the car, remembering. He hadn't known for certain, but this was where he had wanted to go, to the narrow sandy lane leading down to the beach, to the spot where he'd parked a yellow Packard his last night with Marcia. He swung into the lane and the car jounced gently in the sandy ruts. When they reached the knoll overlooking the gulf he stopped the car and shut off the motor. In daylight the spot looked barren and different, and he saw that there was a small cove and a narrow beach concealed from the highway by the rise of sand and a few small wind-withered trees. The Gulf

114

rolled away, blue-gray and limitless. Mist began to collect on the windshield in pin-point drops, and the drops grew fat and slowly dissolved to the cowling. Sara Colvin sat silently, her hands folded in her lap.

Ramsey turned in the seat and looked back toward the highway. A blue and gray station wagon slowed and came to a stop by the end of the lane. Ramsey watched, but Victor didn't get out. There was no need for him to get out, to walk back to them, Ramsey thought; the lane was the only way he could get the Dodge back to the highway, and if he and Sara tried to walk from this place Victor could easily spot them on the flat terrain.

He turned back in the seat, uneasily aware of Sara's quiet presence. He pulled up his shirt and inspected the wound in his side. The cut was a small one and not very deep.

Sara Colvin made a small frightened sound. "Rack— you are hurt."

"Not bad," he said. "Compliments of Sonny." He placed his hands on the wheel and gazed out over the water. Now is the time, he thought, the time for the sweet talk and the pay-off. He was being rushed; he hadn't wanted it this way, but it couldn't be helped now. He turned his head and smiled at her. He hoped the smile appeared sincere. "Well, what now?"

Her lips quivered and her hands went to her face. "I do not know. Rack, I do not know . . ." She sobbed like a little girl.

CHAPTER 16

HE PLACED AN ARM about her shoulders and pulled her gently against him. Presently her sobbing stopped. Silently he handed her a clean handkerchief from the breast pocket of his jacket. She wiped her eyes, sighed brokenly, and sat twisting the handkerchief with her fingers. She made no move to escape his circling arm. He held her a little tighter.

"I—I am sorry," she said. "I have not cried in a long time."

"Cry if you want to." His cheek was against the top of her small head. Her hair held a faint flower fragrance.

"Rack," she said in a low voice, "there is something I must tell you."

"Yes?" He stiffened a little, suddenly alert. "What is it?"

"After what you have done for me, you have a right to know. I—I could not tell you before." She paused, and then said hesitantly, "You—you have wondered about Blake Bowen, have you not? And me?"

He didn't answer. Let her go, he thought. Let her tell it. Now is the time. He patted her arm, encouraging her to go on.

"He means nothing to me, but I—I owed him a debt." She lowered her head, twisted the handkerchief slowly and went on in a low clear voice. "What I tell you is true. Six months ago my agency booked me at the Jungle Tavern. I came to this city from Fort Worth. My money was almost gone and I needed the work. When I arrived here, I was ill, but I tried to dance. I could not finish the last show. I had a high temperature. Blake was very kind to me. He called a doctor. I had pneumonia. Blake paid for the doctor and for the hospital—I was there three weeks. He came to see me every day. When I was well, I danced at the Tavern. It was the least I could do. The patrons semed to like me, and Blake paid well. He would not let me repay him for the medical and hospital expense. When my booking was up, Blake asked me to stay on, offered me more money. I was grateful to him, so I stayed." She paused, twisting the handkerchief.

"Go on," Ramsey said gently.

"One day Blake gave me a sealed package and asked me to take it to the bank for him and put it in a safe deposit box—in my name. I did not understand, but I did it. After that he sent me to the bank almost every week with a package. One day I opened a package and sealed it up again. It was money, lots of money."

Ramsey felt the sudden beating of his heart. He asked carefully, "Did Bowen know that you had opened a package?"

"Yes. I told him. At first he was very angry. I thought he was going to strike me. Then he laughed, and said of

116

course it was money. What else would one put in a bank? He said the money was merely profits from the club and gambling winnings. I asked him why he did not have the deposit box in his own name. He said it was because he did not want to pay income tax on it, that it was a common business practice. I did not clearly understand. He asked me to promise that I would not tell anyone. I promised but I did not like it. From time to time he would ask me to bring money from the box, and I did it—because of what he had done for me." She looked up at him. "Do you believe me, Rack?"

"Yes," he said, thinking that Phil Stark had been right. He had no choice now; he had to go through with it. The money was there, for sure, and he must get it, today, now, as soon as possible. He glanced up at the rear-view mirror. Far back on the highway the station wagon waited patiently, a toy car in the distance. "And that is all Bowen meant to you?" he asked.

"Yes. He was kind to me, and I felt that I should repay him in any way I could."

"He was kind to you for a reason."

"I—I realized that later. He would not let me leave, and he watched me very closely. I became frightened. I did not know what to do. I was almost never alone. Sonny or Rafael, or both of them, would follow me home, to the bank, everywhere I went. I—I had no friends, no one but you, and you had gone away. . . ." Her voice broke.

He held her close. "It's all right now." He began to plan, to scheme. "He can't hurt you now."

"He—he never touched me," she said, "not until today. He was—like a madman. He accused me of telling you about the money in the deposit box. When I denied it he said I lied and he slapped me . . ." He felt her tremble.

"Did he ever—make love to you? Bowen, I mean?"

"Yes—at first. But I discouraged him."

"Like you did me—at first?"

"Yes," she said soberly, "like I have discouraged all men until—until last night." Her eyes were lowered and he saw the faint blush on her cheeks.

He said, "Sara, I hated to leave you last night. It was that damned telephone, Bowen calling you . . ."

"I know." Her voice was almost a whisper. For a moment there was silence in the car and they could hear the

117

soft slapping of the water on the tiny curved beach below them. Then she spoke in a small shy voice. "There are no telephones here."

He had no words. He sat very still, holding her against him.

She said with a faint note of reproach, "And no oil heiresses."

He had hurt her more than he knew, he thought. She was a strange girl, grave and trusting and gentle. She was trusting him now, and he was going to betray her, if he could. He thought about her and about the girl she had called the oil heiress. Marcia. Dead now, cold and dead, with the pulsing life gone out of her body forever. Once more he saw her face in the instant before the bullet had struck her, and he knew that he would see that face until he died.

"Forget the oil heiress," he said, and as he spoke he wondered suddenly if Sara knew yet that Marcia was dead. It was in the papers, and no doubt on the radio . . .

She looked up at him. Her eyes held a soft melting look and the faint flush still touched her ivory skin. "Can I forget her, Rack?"

She doesn't know, he thought. She can't know. For an instant he was tempted to tell her, but he realized immediately that it would weaken his hand. She would know it soon enough, as she would know a number of things. "Of course." He tried to grin. "Anyhow, she's married now."

"Have you forgotten her?"

He nodded, avoiding her eyes, knowing that he lied. He would never forget Marcia. Maybe it had not been love they had had, but it had been something strong and wild and maybe as lasting as love, for all he knew. What the hell was love, anyhow? And how many men had Marcia loved besides Rackwell Ramsey and Jefferson Carr and Blake Bowen and the boy from Dartmouth and God knew who else? Phil Stark, too? He jerked his mind back to the present; he was wasting precious time. "Listen, Sara—I know about that money of Bowen's. It's profits from narcotics—dope. The Jungle Tavern is a clearing house for the stuff. If the federal men check him, as they did last year, they won't find anything—just the club's books. But Bowen needs you to protect his dirty money. He must keep it in a safe place, and in cash, and he can't have it traced to him. You didn't know about the dope?"

118

She shook her head quickly. "Truly, I did not. It is—horrible." She gazed up at him with troubled eyes. "How do you know this, Rack?"

"I know, believe me."

"Who are you?" she asked. "Really? You know this about Blake because you are a—an officer? Perhaps a government agent?"

"No, no," he said impatiently. "Nothing like that. Listen—"

She placed soft fingers over his mouth. "Never mind, Rack. You do not have to explain to me, not now. I trust you, and I—I have a feeling for you, in my heart. And if you did not care for me—a little—you would not have done the thing you did for me today."

He pulled her head against his chest and looked in the mirror once more. The station wagon was still there, up on the highway, and he knew that Victor would warn him somehow if there was trouble. He was safe here, for a while, but he had to finish it, clinch the deal, before he took Sara away from this place. He said, "You can't stay here, not now. Come with me to Wyoming."

She stirred contentedly against him. "Anywhere, Rack, if you want me."

He tilted her chin and her mouth came up to meet his. Her lips were soft and hot and again he sensed the abandonment in her, maybe an awakening, and inside of him, beneath the trouble and the worry and desperateness, he felt a strange and confusing tenderness, and odd sense of possessiveness. And suddenly he pushed her away, almost roughly. "Sara, I—"

"Do not talk," she whispered. "Do not worry yourself. I—I love you, Rack. I admit it, shamelessly. I loved you the first time I saw you. I do not know how I knew, but I did, and I think you feel a little of what I feel. Is it not so?"

"Yes," he said uneasily.

"You have been lonely as I have been lonely," she murmured. "You have asked me to go with you, and I will be happy and proud to go, wherever you say."

He kissed her again, and it came to him then, the plan, and it sprouted and bloomed. It was better than Phil Stark's plan, he thought. He knew how he could get her to give him Blake Bowen's money. He pushed her gently away. "Sara, we've got to talk."

119

Her eyes were bewildered, and he tried not to look at them. "Yes. About the money in the deposit box. We can't just go away and leave it. You are the only one who can get it. Have you thought of that?"

"No," she said soberly. "I have not."

"Do you have the key?"

"Yes. Blake took the one I had in my purse, but I have another at the apartment. As I told you, the box is in my name, and I must sign a register each time I open it. But—"

"We must get the money," he said quickly, "and turn it over to the police, before we leave. That is the right thing to do."

She frowned. "But why? The money does not concern us. If you wish, after we are gone, we can write the police . . ."

He shook his head impatiently. "No. This has to be settled before we leave." He touched her cheek and smiled. "Can't you see? I want everything between you and Bowen wiped off the books. If it isn't, it will follow us, wherever we go, and maybe cause trouble for you. After all, in the eyes of the law you are an accomplice."

"That is true," she said in a troubled voice. "I had not thought of it in that way. You think we should get the money, go to the police together and explain?"

He nodded. "Then we can be free. We'll go to Wyoming and—"

"Must we go there?" She was suddenly smiling, bright-eyed. "You are right, Rack, about the money. It is our duty. But I have thought I would like it in California."

He shrugged, thinking dismally that it didn't matter—California, Kalamazoo, the Belgian Congo or Scipio Siding, Ohio. "Maybe they need derrick riggers in California, too."

She laughed softly. "I think I am very happy. Are you happy, Rack?"

"Yes." He gazed out over the Gulf. The mist had cleared and for the first time he realized that a foggy yellow sun was shining through the gray clouds. It made the air hot and muggy and he tugged at the knot of his tie. There wasn't any breeze, and the water lapped sluggishly on the shore. "We'll get married," he said, but he couldn't look

120

at her. It sounded phony, even to him; surely she would sense the falseness.

Tears appeared on her lashes and her lips trembled. "I do not expect that. Please do not think that you must ask me. Later, perhaps, we will talk about it. But now I must ask a favor. It is important to me, and you are the only person who can grant it."

"Sara," he said helplessly, "I—"

"Please," she said quickly. "Please understand. It is something I have decided. It is time for me to abide by my own feelings. This favor I ask is very important to me. It will prove that I have grown up, that I am a complete woman, that I have the courage to follow my heart. There have been no other men for me. I—I want you to be the first. Please, Rack."

"No others?" he asked. "Ever?"

"No. It is the truth."

He looked away. The Judas feeling was strong, but there was another feeling, and he would not name it. He didn't try to name it. He knew there would be no walking hand in hand to the police with a bundle of dirty dope money and no trip to California and no wedding, for God's sake. Soon she would know that he was really dirt and after it was over, after this time by the gulf, she would know what he was. He pulled her to him roughly and his mouth drove against hers. His hands went over her body and she pressed against him, her face hot against his. "Here?" he whispered. "Here in the car?"

"No, no." Her voice was faint. "On the beach, near the water."

The water, he thought, in an odd detached way, the beginning and the end of the universe. He had learned it in high school; nothing could live without water, not even a blade of grass, and maybe Sara Colvin sensed it in her soul, the desire to live and be a woman, near the water. He slid out of the car, moved around to her side and opened the door. He didn't look toward the highway, but he knew that Victor was still there, waiting. Soon it would be over, one way or the other.

He walked with her across the sand and held her hand as they descended the little hill to the small hidden cove and the tiny beach. He spread his coat on the damp sand and they lay together beneath the misty saffron sky. They

121

were in a little private world of their own and the only sound was the gentle lapping of the waves on the sand a few feet away.

He did not hurry and was very gentle, because he was a little awed and aware of his responsibility to her, and for a brief time he forgot why he came to be there and what the rest of the day held in store for him. He kissed her lips and her flushed cheeks and her throat, and she murmured something in Spanish he did not understand. And presently he came to know that she had indeed told him the truth; no other man had ever known her as he was knowing her now.

CHAPTER 17

SHE CRIED A LITTLE when they were back in the car, but she smiled at him. "Do not pay any attention to my tears. I am very happy." She looked away shyly. "Perhaps I—I am not all that you would like me to be, but I will learn, if you will teach me."

He was back in the present again, fighting his thoughts. The station wagon still waited at the end of the lane. Sara Colvin touched his hand. "I have a proud feeling, a good feeling. Everything is right now. Let us get the money and give it to the police. Then we will be—free."

"Yes," he said, starting the motor of the Dodge. He backed around in the sand and headed slowly up the lane. "To your apartment?"

"Yes. I will get a few clothes and the key."

"We'll have to hurry—they'll be hunting for us."

She said soberly, "There is danger, is there not?"

"Maybe."

"Then why do we not go to the police now? We can tell them about the money, and give them the key." She touched his arm. "Would not that be better?"

He thought fast. It would be better, indeed—but not for him. The police would be delighted to see him; whatever help he gave them in exposing a dope peddler would

122

not excuse him from the charge of murder. Neither he nor Phil Stark would gain, and Stark would still hold the incriminating gun and letter. He had to deliver Blake Bowen's money to Phil Stark. There was no other choice. "There isn't time for that," he said shortly. "There is no telling what they'll do. Bowen may send someone to the bank for the money and—"

"No," she said quickly. "He cannot. Only I have access to the deposit box. The people at the bank told me."

His brain raced wildly. "But we must have proof," he said harshly. "Please, Sara, you've got to trust me."

"I trust you, Rack," she said gravely. "Do not mention trust. Perhaps I do not fully understand, but it is just that I worry about the danger—for you. You have already risked much for me today, and I have learned how cruel Blake can be. The police can go with us to the bank, and I will show them—"

"No," he almost shouted.

She looked at him in surprise. Then she touched his arm. "All right, Rack. You are—are wrought up. It was only a suggestion, but you know best. It does not matter—as long as we can go away afterward."

"We will," he said, feeling the cold sweat of relief on his forehead. "Just trust me, Sara."

They reached the end of the lane and as he swung the car out onto the highway he shot a glance at Victor behind the wheel of the station wagon. For an instant their eyes met. Victor winked, and Ramsey knew that he'd seen him and Sara leave the car and go down to the beach. He hoped Sara had not seen the wink, and he shot a sidelong glance at her, but she was gazing thoughtfully at the road ahead and had apparently paid no attention to a fat man sitting in a parked station wagon.

They didn't talk much during the ride back to the city. Once she asked him for a cigarette and smiled as he held the dash lighter for her. There was a soft color to her cheeks and her dark eyes held a depth and brightness he had not noticed before. After they reached the city it took them almost thirty minutes in the traffic to reach her apartment building. He left the motor running and told her to hurry. She nodded silently and ran inside. After she was gone, he had some bad moments. What if she took it upon herself to call the police, after all? What if she didn't come

123

back to him? He glanced nervously up and down the street. The passing cars were just cars, with men and women and children riding in them. Just ordinary people going about their ordinary business. No police cruisers, no sirens, no Sonny and Rafael. Not yet. He turned on the car's radio and heard a news announcer's smooth voice:

. . . new developments in the murder of Mrs. Jefferson Carr. Police have reported that an anonymous telephone caller has informed them that the killer of Mrs. Carr is a man named Rackwell Ramsey, an oil field worker currently registered at the Gulf Hotel of this city. Ramsey was described as an alleged former suitor of Mrs. Carr before her marriage to Mr. Carr. The unknown informer said that jealousy was the motive for the murder and that Ramsey is about thirty years old, weighing between one hundred and eighty and two hundred pounds, six foot tall, gray eyes, blond hair cut short, and wearing when last seen a gray flannel suit, tan raincoat and a dark brown felt hat. This description corresponds to one given police earlier today by a taxi driver of a stranger he drove to the fashionable Carr residence on the gulf road shortly before the shooting last night. Police traced the call to a telephone booth in the Western Bus Terminal, but there the trail ended. They have reason to believe that the person who made the call is the same person who called them last night immediately after Mrs. Carr was shot. Stay tuned to this station for—"

Ramsey turned off the radio, feeling sweat on his temples. He heard a step on the sidewalk close by. He swung his head quickly, his hand on the gun beside him. Victor leaned in the open window of the Dodge. His pipe was in his mouth and the rich aroma of the burning tobacco filled the car. His broad fat face seemed to sag, and his eyes were slits between red lids. He said, "I saw her go in. Is she going to get the money for you?"

Ramsey nodded, his lips compressed.

"Good work. Phil will be pleased."

"To hell with Phil. I just heard on the radio that the cops even have my name now. What is this—a double-double frame?"

Victor sighed. "I don't know about your private life. All I know is that Phil didn't tip off the cops. Why should he? But somebody did." He sighed again, puffed on the pipe,

124

and said gravely, "You're getting hotter by the second, boy."

Ramsey gripped the wheel and watched the apartment entrance.

Victor said, "Don't go back to the Gulf Hotel. The cops are waiting for you there." He hesitated, puffing slowly. Then he said, "Uh—what happened at Bowen's place?"

"I rescued the girl," Ramsey said bitterly, "just like in the movies. I shot Bowen in the leg and knocked Sonny and Rafael cold. I was a goddamned hero."

Victor said, "I—uh—wanted to help you, but Phil don't pay me for any rough stuff."

"To hell with you."

Victor peered at him. "You and the girl was down on the beach quite a while."

"I was clinching the deal."

"Nice work."

"Shut the hell up."

"No offense," Victor said. "Are you going to the bank now?"

"As soon as she comes out. She's getting the key to the deposit box and packing some clothes. We'll get the money and go to the airport. She thinks we're going to turn the money over to the police and walk hand in hand into the sunset. I'll ditch her while she's buying the tickets and take the money to Stark." He looked at Victor and said evenly, "Does that meet with your approval, you goddamned stooge?"

Victor said sadly, "Do you have to do it that way?"

"How the hell else can I do it? Go away. I don't want you around when she comes out."

Victor took the pipe from his mouth and gazed at the bowl. His chin quivered a little. "You called me a stooge," he said, "and maybe I am. But that's my job. Can't you see that?"

"It's a hell of a job."

"Listen," Victor said earnestly, "two years ago I was carrying a mail route. I was satisfied to keep on carrying mail and wait for my pension. Then my oldest boy got polio. My daughter broke her leg on the school playground. Then my other boy, the baby, had to have his appendix out. Then my wife had a miscarriage—she was in the hospital eight weeks and damn near died. My '38 Chevvy burned out a main bearing and I got behind on my mortgage payments. It all happened at once, and I was just about nuts. Then one night after bowling with the post office team I went with some of the boys to the Starlight Club to have a beer and maybe play the nickel slots a little. I got to talking to Phil Stark, and he offered me a job. Three times the money I made at the post office. I'm getting along fine now. That Ford station wagon will be mine after three more payments, and I got my house almost paid for. My kids get shoes when they need 'em, my wife can buy a new dress once in a while, and we eat good. We got a TV and beer in a new refrigerator. I owe it all to Phil Stark. He's been square with me, and I'll be square with him."

"Very touching," Ramsey said. "True blue Victor."

Victor sighed. "I don't blame you for being sore about this. But Phil will keep his word to you."

"Go away."

Victor gazed at him soberly. "Don't get any ideas. I'll see you at the bank." He withdrew his head and moved away.

Ramsey drummed nervous fingers on the wheel. What was keeping Sara? Abruptly he got out of the car and crossed to the apartment building entrance. He lit a cigarette and gazed up and down the street. Down near the corner he saw Victor's Ford parked at the curb. Other cars moved slowly past. The sun was gone and leaden clouds were floating slowly across the sky. It's going to rain again, he thought. Then he made up his mind, turned and entered the building. The telephone booth door was open. He gazed at the booth, remembering with a rush the events of the last two days. The booth seemed to beckon him. He entered the booth, closed the door, thumbed the book, dropped a coin and dialed the Gulf Hotel. As he waited, he watched the elevator.

A female voice spoke in his ear. "Good afternoon—the Gulf Hotel."

"This is the police department," Ramsey said gruffly. "We're doing some routine checking. Last night there was a telephone message for a Mr. Rackwell Ramsey, who is registered there. Do you have a record of it?"

"The police? Really, I don't know if I should—"

"This is important," Ramsey snapped, "and I'm in a hurry. Please call the manager."

"Oh, no," the voice said hastily, "that won't be necessary. We keep carbons of all messages. Did you say the name was Ramsey?"

"Yes."

"Just a moment, please."

He waited, his fingers gripping the receiver, and watched the elevator. She should be coming down any second now, he thought, and looked at his wrist watch. After three o'clock in the afternoon. He had lost all track of time. It seemed a week ago that he had followed Sonny and Rafael and Sara to the Jungle Tavern. The voice spoke in his ear. "I have it. Mr. Rackwell Ramsey, Room 220. The name is so unusual—Rackwell. Hey—he's in the papers! He murdered that woman!"

"Were you on duty when the call came in?" Ramsey asked coldly.

"Yes, I was," the voice said excitedly. "I remember it very well. I work from three to eleven. They said to have Mr. Ramsey call a Texas exchange, four, nine, nine—"

"Was it a man or a woman who called?" Ramsey cut in.

"It was a woman. She had a very nice voice. I typed the message and gave it to the clerk, and—"

"Thank you." Through the glass Ramsey saw Sara Colvin step out of the elevator. He hung up quickly and left the booth. Sara's high heels clicked on the marble floor as she moved to the door. Ramsey called to her. She stopped and turned, her eyes startled. Then she smiled. As he went to her, he thought of what the switchboard girl at the Gulf Hotel had told him. It had been a woman who had set the trap for him at Marcia's house. Sara? Marcia? Not Marcia, because she was dead . . . Who? What other woman did he know except Sara?

He tried to smile at her. "All ready?" She had changed her torn dress for a dark blue tailored suit and a small blue hat. Her traveling outfit, he thought; maybe she considers it her wedding outfit. But she wasn't going far, only as far as the airport, and there wouldn't be any wedding. In each hand she held a medium-sized leather bag, one black, one brown.

She said breathlessly, "I am sorry I was so long, Rack, but I did not have my key and I had to find the superin-

127

tendent, and it was a problem deciding what to take with me. I had to leave most of my clothes and all my costumes and my record player. The superintendent said he'd store them for me."

He took the bags from her. One was heavy, the other light.

"My clothes are in the black one," she said. "The other is empty."

He nodded in approval. "Smart girl. Come on."

He put the bags in the back seat of the Dodge. As they drove away she looked back at the small neat apartment house. "Goodbye," she said softly and lifted a hand.

"Sorry to leave?" In the rear-view mirror he saw Victor's station wagon pull away from the curb and follow them.

"Not really," she said. "It is just that it has been home to me for a long time."

"We'll find a new home," he said, not caring any more. "A better one."

She moved up against him.

"What bank?" he asked.

"The Seaboard National . . . Are we doing the right thing, Rack? About the money?"

"It's the only way."

"I—I am a little frightened."

He patted her knee. "Don't be. It'll soon be over." He turned a corner and headed for the business district.

"Would—would it not be better if we went to the police first?"

"No," he said sharply.

The Seaboard National Bank was housed in a big sandstone building on a corner opposite a mammoth chain drug store. Ramsey circled the block twice before he found a place to park close to the bank entrance. He got out, put a penny in the parking meter and opened the car door. He tried to smile at Sara, but his lips felt stiff. "All right," he said.

She gazed at him, her eyes big and dark in her small pale face. "Please do not worry," she said softly. "I will be quick." She lifted the brown bag from the rear seat and walked briskly to the bank's glittering bronze and glass doors. She turned and gave him a tremulous smile. He

128

lifted a hand. She entered the bank then, and the doors swung gently behind her. Something twisted in his stomach.

He got back into the Dodge and gripped the wheel with sweaty palms. He lit a cigarette. So far, so good, he thought. No Rafael and Sonny yet, and he wondered about it. Surely they would have watched Sara's apartment, knowing that she would probably return there. And Bowen would guess that he, Ramsey, would take Sara to the bank. He would be a fool not to guess it. Maybe that was why they had waited—until Sara had the money. They couldn't get it without her. Ramsey felt a chill across his shoulders. He turned in the seat, gazed about. The street was clogged with cars and trucks, and people swarmed along the sidewalks. A policeman stood on the corner in front of the drug store, laughing and talking with a tanned man wearing high-heeled boots and a creamy Stetson. The rain had started again, more of a mist than rain, and nobody seemed to be paying any attention to it. Then he saw Victor coming through the crowd.

The fat man poked his head in the car window.

"Go away," Ramsey snarled.

"Take it easy. It's almost over."

"Where are Bowen's boys?" Ramsey asked. "I can't figure it out."

"Neither can I," the fat man admitted soberly. "I thought sure they'd be on your tail before now." He shot an apprehensive glance up and down the street.

"They're waiting until she has the money," Ramsey said. "Then they'll move in."

"Don't talk like that," Victor said sharply. His fat face was suddenly pale. "I gotta go with you."

"Go with me?"

Victor nodded gloomily. "Phil's orders. He said when you get the money I should stay with you until it's delivered to him."

"So he don't trust me?"

Victor didn't answer. He opened the car door and got into the rear seat.

"How'll I explain you to the girl?" Ramsey asked.

"I don't know. That's up to you." Victor sighed heavily. "Does it make any difference now?"

"Shut up," Ramsey said bitterly. He took the gun from

129

the seat and dropped it into the right pocket of his coat. Then he sat with his hands on the wheel watching the bank entrance, sweating in his own private little hell.

CHAPTER 18

SHE CAME OUT of the bank carrying the brown bag. Ramsey leaned over, opened the car door and took the bag from her. It felt surprisingly light. How much did a hundred thousand dollars weigh? He tossed the bag to the rear seat beside Victor and put the Dodge in gear. He saw Sara gazing at the fat man, her expression bewildered, and he said quickly, "He's a friend, Sara. He's going to help us."

"But—"

"I'll explain later," Ramsey said sharply. He leaned across her and slammed the door.

He heard her quick intake of breath. "Rack!"

He followed her stricken gaze. Sonny and Rafael were running toward them. There was a patch of adhesive tape on Sonny's face. In his haste he bumped into a stout woman carrying a full shopping bag. They both sprawled to the sidewalk amidst spilled cans and assorted groceries. Rafael kept coming, an intent vicious look on his lean brown face. Are they crazy? Ramsey thought wildly. They can't do it here, not with all these people. He began to jockey the Dodge out of the parking space, twisting the wheel.

Rafael reached the car and a thin brown hand clawed at the door handle. Sara quickly flicked a button which locked the door. She shrank back against Ramsey. Rafael's head and shoulders were inside the car, a hand reaching across Sara for the ignition key. Victor leaned forward from the rear seat and flicked the barrel of a revolver in a short arc against the bridge of Rafael's thin hawk nose. Rafael groaned and jerked back, his hand to his nose. But his head stayed inside the car. Victor hit him again. Rafael staggered backward across the sidewalk. A woman screamed.

Ramsey glanced back once, and then shot the Dodge

130

out into the traffic. He heard another scream and men shouting. Brakes screeched behind him, and a police whistle shrilled. He kept going, gaining speed. At the corner the light was red. Cars were drifting across the intersection in a steady stream. Ramsey picked a hole and roared through. More screeching of brakes, and an outraged symphony of horns. But he was through.

"Where are they?" he snapped at Sara.

She was looking back. "I—I do not see them."

"Police?"

"No."

"Step on it!" Victor yelled.

He fed gas, weaving between the cars. Two blocks from the bank he swung into an alley. It was a narrow alley, brick-paved. Ahead of them a pick-up truck began to back away from a loading platform. Ramsey pressed the horn, the sound blasting his ears in the alley's narrow confines. The truck stopped dead, and the Dodge skimmed past. Ahead was a solid brick wall and a sign. *Dead End*. Ramsey cut the wheel and locked the brakes. The Dodge shuddered and swerved, and another sign loomed up. *One Way*. An arrow pointed right. The Dodge was now headed left. An oncoming car jerked toward the wall. The driver shouted wildly as the Dodge roared past. Ramsey heard the thin scream of metal scraping the wall.

Abruptly the alley ended. Ramsey saw cars zipping past on the street. He slammed on the brakes. The sedan's nose dipped downward and Sara braced herself against the dash. Behind him Ramsey heard Victor grunt as the fat man lurched forward off the rear seat. The Dodge swung into the street. A pale green convertible skittered away like a frightened colt. The Dodge straightened out, gathered speed. Ramsey thought he heard the sound of a siren, but he wasn't certain. It could have been the blood singing in his ears. Two blocks, four blocks, six, the lights all green. Then a long ramp leading up to an express highway. The Dodge sped up the ramp and merged with the three-lane line of cars headed west. Ramsey held the car at an even sixty.

Sara Colvin and Victor were looking back.

"See anything?"

"Just cars," Victor said. "No cops yet. Keep going."

Ramsey spoke to Sara. "The airport is the next stop. You get two tickets for Los Angeles."

"Rack, remember the police, and the money."

"We'll call them from the airport—as soon as we see about a plane."

"But if we went to the police now . . ."

"We can't," Ramsey snapped. "It's too late for that. Sonny and Rafael are after us. We can't depend on the police. Our only chance now is to get out of Texas. We'd better leave the money at the airport office. The police can pick it up. We'll figure it out . . ." He kept talking, to keep her from asking questions, and he hardly knew what he said.

Victor sat silently, staring out the rear window. Sara looked at him and then at Ramsey, but she made no comment. Ramsey was glad when he saw the tower of the airport. He swung the car off the highway and down to the huge parking area beside the landing strips. Overhead a silver plane circled into the wind for a landing. A loud-speaker crackled with a voice announcing arrivals and departures of the various flights. *Flight Four for Mexico City now loading at gate six . . .* Ramsey stopped the Dodge in a vacant space in a long row of parked cars. He took out his wallet and handed Sara all the money he had left. "Get tickets for Los Angeles or anywhere west—just so it's soon. I'll wait here."

She looked at the money he had given her. "But, Rack, I have money for the tickets. I drew out my savings account when I was in the bank—over three hundred dollars."

"Take it," he said harshly. "Hurry."

She looked at him, her eyes troubled, and she glanced at Victor sitting silently in the rear seat. "Who are you?" she asked gravely. "Why are you with us?"

Victor stirred uncomfortably. "Uh—I'm just a friend, like he said. I—uh—" He looked at Ramsey imploringly.

Ramsey said quickly, "Sara, it's all right. Please trust me. Hurry and get the tickets." He smiled at her. "I'll explain about Victor when you come back."

She hesitated. He could not tell what her thoughts were. Then she said, "All right, Rack," and got out of the car. She hesitated a moment, gazing in at him. Ramsey kept the smile frozen on his lips. Victor turned his head and peered

132

out of the car's rear window. Abruptly the girl walked away toward the airport office. Ramsey watched her until her small figure was out of sight among the parked cars. He thought, *Goodbye, honey. This is the end of the line.*

Victor said, "That little girl smells a rat. Let's get out of here." He lifted the brown bag to the front seat, got out and opened the door. "Move over. I'll drive."

Ramsey slid over and placed the bag on his knees while Victor got behind the wheel. Ramsey tapped the bag. "Maybe we'd better open it."

"Yeah," Victor grunted. "But hurry."

Ramsey released the metal catches, lifted the brown leather lid. They stared at the green mass of bills tied in neat bundles. Victor's eyes widened, and he ran his tongue over his lips. Ramsey snapped the bag shut. He felt old and tired and sick. His head still ached and the shallow wound in his side burned with a puckered dryness. As Victor drove the car away from the airport, Ramsey looked back once. Sara Colvin was not in sight. She's still inside, he thought, arranging for passage west for two. She would come back to where the car had been and he would be gone, and the bag of money would be gone. She would know for certain then, and there was nothing he could do about it.

They turned out on the highway and gathered speed. Ramsey fingered the bag on his knees and gazed at the flat country in the misty drizzle and at the black wet road ahead. The Judas feeling was riding him hard, and suddenly he thought he may as well be a complete Judas, not a reluctant one, and he remembered the time with Sara by the water in the saffron sunlight. He had nothing much to lose any more, he thought. Why not go whole hog? He tapped the brown bag and said softly to Victor, "There's a hundred thousand dollars here."

Victor swallowed and kept his eyes on the road. "I saw it."

"And here we are, just the two of us."

"Yes." Victor shot Ramsey a furtive sidelong glance. "I've thought about it, don't think I haven't."

"We're headed west," Ramsey said softly. "Let's just keep going."

Victor swallowed again. He didn't speak.

133

"A hundred thousand," Ramsey said, watching him. "Split two ways."

Victor didn't answer for a moment. Then he said in a strained voice, "I can't. I—I just can't. I got a wife, and kids . . ."

"You can send for them. Start a new life, with fifty thousand bucks that nobody will ever dare claim. That kind of money will buy plenty of shoes for your kids." As he spoke Ramsey felt detached and completely evil.

"No," Victor said hoarsely. There were globules of sweat on his fat face. "Phil has played square with me. I can't double-cross him. And he made a deal with you. He'll stand by his word."

"A murder deal," Ramsey said. "A frame." He looked at Victor. "I don't need you. I can take off by myself. Why should I split with anyone?"

Victor shot him a frightened glance. "You wouldn't do that," he said shrilly.

"Why the hell not? I've got a gun. I can dump you out right now and keep right on going."

Victor's face paled. "N-now, listen," he stuttered. "You're talking crazy. You wouldn't get very far. And remember the—the evidence Phil's got. If you skipped, he'd turn it over to the cops, and—"

Ramsey laughed. "Hell, the cops will shoot me on sight anyhow. I couldn't be any hotter." He took the Colt .38 from his coat pocket and held it on top of the bag, so that Victor could see it. "I've got nothing to lose, and maybe I'll gain a hundred thousand dollars. I could scoot across the Border and live good for a long time."

The fat man was torn between watching the road and the gun in Ramsey's hand. "Don't talk like that," he pleaded. "You done fine, up until now. Don't spoil it." His eyes rolled toward the gun. "P-put that thing away."

"How do I know Stark will keep his word?"

"He will, he will," Victor said quickly. "I promise you. He's a square shooter and I give you my word—"

"Oh, shut up." Ramsey was disgusted with himself for his childish action. He knew that he was just needling Victor, and that he wouldn't have a chance if he tried to run with the money. His only chance, if he had a chance, was with Phil Stark. His goading of Victor had been pure malice, a kind of release and a protest after the tension and the fear of the past twenty-four hours. He was ashamed and put the gun back in his pocket.

Victor sighed heavily and pulled a meaty hand down over his fat damp face. He swallowed and muttered, "Rain starting again." He turned on the windshield wipers with a hand that shook a little. The Dodge droned along, the wipers swishing softly. The flat plains of the gulf coast were all around them and the road stretched wide and empty. Through the rain the sky was thick and gray, except for a single yellow ray of sunshine on the far horizon.

Ramsey thought of Sara Colvin, of the sweet tender time on the beach. He remembered her glad, proud tears and her gentle voice with the illusive accent: *I have a proud feeling, a good feeling. Everything is right now . . .* She was waiting for him now, back at the airport. What would happen to her when Bowen's men found her, with the money gone? And they would surely find her. What then? He felt a little sick, and he knew why he had goaded Victor, an easy-going fat man who had once carried the United States mail, and who was also trapped and beaten, even if he did have a television set and beer in a new refrigerator.

The flat empty country rolled past. Suddenly Ramsey knew that it was too quiet, too peaceful. It had all been too easy. He had an uneasy feeling, a kind of black warning of danger. He turned in the seat and looked back. Far down the road behind them was a lone car. It grew bigger as he watched, and he knew that it was coming fast. He narrowed his eyes, trying to see more clearly in the rain. The car was big and low and from the front silhouette he guessed it to be a Cadillac, a late model. He snapped at Victor, "Does Blake Bowen own a black Cadillac?"

"Yes." Victor glanced at Ramsey with worried eyes. "He's got a Jaguar, too, and this Dodge. Why?"

"A black Caddy is on our tail and gaining. Step on it."

Victor gulped and gripped the wheel. The Dodge leaped ahead. The motor sang a new song and the tires hummed louder on the wet asphalt. But the car behind continued to gain. Ramsey could see the forms of two persons in the front seat. "Faster," he said to Victor.

"Doing eighty-five now." Victor was panting, as if he were personally providing the car's power. "It ain't far to the club now." The Dodge's speed subtly increased. "Can we shake 'em?"

"No," Ramsey said sharply. "They're coming up behind."

"Who?" Victor's scared eyes were on the road rushing at them.

"Sonny and Rafael, I think."

"Ninety," Victor panted. "Ninety-two, I mean . . ."

Ramsey took the gun from his pocket and rolled down the window. Victor rolled his eyes at him. "No shooting!" he cried. "Nothing like that!"

The windshield cracked with a splintering sound and damp air rushed through a jagged hole. In the same instant Ramsey saw a smaller hole in the rear window. Victor yelled something, and the car swerved dangerously.

"Keep it on the road!" Ramsey yelled. He pushed the brown bag to the floor, leaned out the window, the gun in his left hand. The wind whipped his face and carried his hat back into the car. Except for the pursuing Cadillac, the road was clear. In the wind he squinted along the barrel of the .38 and pulled the trigger. The gun bucked in his hand and bitter powder smoke swept past his face. One of the men in the car behind was also leaning out a window, on the right side. The man's arm went up and down. A sound like an angry bee buzzed past Ramsey's face. Ramsey fired again and then ducked inside, his head against the back of the seat. Victor's fat shoulders hunched low over the wheel and his head was pulled down. Above the sound of speed and the wind something went *thunk* in the back of the Dodge. Victor flinched and tried to get his head lower. The car faltered for a moment and then roared ahead.

Ramsey raised his head. The Cadillac was close now, closing in, maybe fifty yards behind. Ramsey leaned far out, holding the gun in his right hand this time, steadying it with his left. He aimed and fired, while the wind clawed at his face. He fired again. And again.

With shocking suddenness the front wheels of the Cadillac buckled. The big car swung sideways across the road. Then it straightened for an instant and the fin-tailed rear whipped around and the car leaped for the shallow ditch. It rolled over twice, an awesome sight, and chunks of wet Texas earth shot high into the sky. Then Victor

136

wheeled the Dodge around a curve and the scene behind was gone.

Ramsey sank back against the seat, still holding the gun. Victor shot him a quick glance, but he said nothing. Ramsey sucked in his breath and closed his eyes. A sickening thought had struck him: *Had they found Sara at the airport? Had she been in the car with them? He had seen only two persons, but she could have been in the rear, maybe on the floor* . . . He groaned aloud. Victor shot him an uneasy glance. "Take it easy. We're almost home."

Ramsey didn't hear him. Maybe she was back there, he thought. Maybe she was dead. Because of him. And if she wasn't dead, he knew what Blake Bowen and Sonny and Rafael would do to her. He knew she had told him the truth. In his urgency he hadn't bothered to ask himself if he believed her story of the trap Bowen had caught her in, that she had not known about the dope. He should have known that she would not lie to him, not after the time on the beach. But he had thought only of himself, of his own skin. And now . . .

All he wanted was to get this over with, this thing he had to do. Then he could go far away and work and drink and forget and maybe it would be a little like it used to be, before he'd come to this city, before he'd lost Pete Davos. But he knew that nothing would ever be the same again. What had Marcia said that first night? *I know I'm cheap, but there's nobody but me to care.* And she had lifted her glass to him. *Hi, brother heel.*

Marcia had understood about him, because she had been like him. Sara had understood, too, maybe in a different way. And with the thought of Sara there came pain and a bitter self-reproach, and for the first time in many years, excepting the time he'd stood over Pete's grave by the mahogany forest, he said a silent prayer, a prayer for Sara Colvin, who had remembered an aunt's pious teachings—until she had met a man named Rackwell Ramsey.

Victor said, "Here we are."

Up ahead Ramsey saw the Starlight Club, looking squat and drab in the gray afternoon. Victor swung the Dodge into the garage and parked beside the blue Cadillac. He got out quickly and pulled down the overhead door. Then he turned to Ramsey and mopped his face with a handker-

137

chief. "Do you—uh—think they're dead?" He jerked his head back toward the highway.

Ramsey didn't answer.

"Snap out of it," Victor said. "You did real good. They was shooting at us, and . . . and . . ." He moved a fat hand in a futile gesture. "I mean, don't feel bad. They was just a couple of hoods, one of 'em a killer—that Rafael. And the kid's a dipso, and a little queer besides. Honest, the cops should give you a medal." He opened the door of the station wagon. "Come on," he said nervously, "let's get it over with."

Ramsey got out.

Victor hesitated, embarrassment on his face. "Look—maybe you better give me that gun you got."

Silently Ramsey handed it over. Victor took it, avoiding Ramsey's gaze, and moved to the door in the wall. Ramsey said bitterly, "Are you going to trust me to bring the money?"

Victor paused, looking sheepish. He snapped his fingers. "Oh, yeah—bring it, will you?"

Ramsey took the brown bag from the Dodge. As he did so, he saw the black bag containing Sara's clothes lying on the rear seat. It looked oddly small and alone. He turned away, carrying the brown bag, feeling a little sick, and followed Victor through the door.

In the dim passageway Victor said in a hoarse whisper, "Now, don't you worry. Phil will be tickled, and everything will be fine."

CHAPTER 19

PHIL STARK WAS not alone in his elegant office. Another man sat slumped in one of the deep red leather chairs, a cold-eyed man with a narrow black mustache and a dark gray suit. Mr. Jefferson Webster Carr, attorney-at-law, the husband of the dead Marcia, sad and remote in his grief. When he saw Ramsey, his thin lips began to work and he started to get out of the chair.

Stark stopped him with an easy gesture. "Now, Jeff, don't upset yourself. I'll handle this."

Carr sank back, but his eyes did not leave Ramsey's face. Ramsey, holding Sara's brown leather bag, stood before the desk. He was aware that Victor was behind him.

Stark spoke pleasantly to Victor. "Any trouble?"

"A little," Ramsey heard Victor say. "But we made it."

"What kind of trouble?" Stark asked sharply. "Did anyone follow you here?"

"They—uh—tried to, but we shook 'em off."

Stark smiled thinly. "All right, Victor. You can tell me about it later." He turned to Ramsey, nodded at the bag. "You have the money?"

"Yes."

"Good, good." Stark rubbed his hands together with a dry sound. "Put it on the desk, please."

"In a minute." Ramsey jerked his head at Jefferson Carr. "What's he doing here?"

Annoyance crossed Stark's smooth, ruddy face. Then he said smoothly, "Mr. Carr is an old friend. He arrived here from Austin early this morning and learned of his wife's death." He hesitated, cleared his throat delicately, and said, "I might add that he is now aware that you are wanted in connection with her murder."

"Who tipped off the police?" Ramsey asked bluntly. "Who phoned in my name, description and address?"

Stark lifted his shoulders. "How would I know that?" He held out a hand. "The bag, please."

"Who called the cops in the first place?" Ramsey asked. "They got there real fast—almost before Victor got me away."

Stark's gaze flicked to Victor and then back to Ramsey. He said harshly, "I'm not good at riddles. What does it matter? All of us here know that you killed Mrs. Carr. Why do you quibble so? I should think that you would be grateful to us."

Jefferson Carr lurched forward in the chair. "Good Christ, Phil! He—he killed Marcia. How can you expect me to—?"

"Please," Stark cut in. "Control yourself, Jeff." He turned to Ramsey and smiled. "I asked Mr. Carr to come here. I am sure that you can sympathize with his agitation. I have told him of my arrangement with you, and he has

139

agreed—under the circumstances—not to interfere. Apparently his natural emotions have temporarily overcome him." He glanced at Carr with a slight expression of distaste. The lawyer was now leaning back in the chair, a hand over his eyes, breathing heavily. ·

"Why did he agree?" Ramsey asked. "Because he owes you twenty thousand dollars—that his wife refused to pay for him?"

"Mr. Carr's reasons do not concern you," Stark said in a clipped voice. Again he held out a hand. "The bag, Ramsey."

Ramsey looked from Stark to Jefferson Carr and back to Stark. He said slowly, "I don't get it; Carr thinks that I killed his wife, and yet he just sits there because you told him to, and because he's an old friend of yours and you happen to have a private deal with me. What the hell kind of a man is that?"

Stark smiled, showing the beautiful gold inlays in his false teeth, and spread his hands. "Be realistic, Ramsey. We're all civilized, intelligent people. Mr. Carr regards you with loathing, I am certain, and his sorrow is great. But nothing will bring back his wife. He understands the situation, and there is no need for—for dramatics."

Ramsey felt a tightness in his throat. Stark wasn't bothering to be very subtle about it. The gambler knew that he had Ramsey trapped. Ramsey said, "You saw Marcia Carr last night—before I arrived."

Stark's eyes narrowed a bit. "Did she tell you?"

"Yes. She also told me that Carr owes you a gambling debt. You wanted her to pay it and she refused."

"What else did she tell you?" Stark said quietly. "Before you killed her?"

"She said Jeff Carr maneuvered her into marrying him, and that she intended to divorce him. And I didn't kill her."

For a moment there was silence. Jefferson Carr stirred in his chair and gazed stonily at the tips of his black polished shoes. Stark shot Carr a sharp, curious glance, and then said to Ramsey, "So Marcia was going to divorce Jeff, eh?"

Ramsey nodded.

"And then marry you, perhaps?"

Ramsey shrugged. "Maybe. We didn't discuss it. . . . What did you do, after she refused to pay Jeff's debt?"

140

"Returned here," Stark snapped. "My business with Mrs. Carr doesn't concern you, and I don't have to explain—"

"Listen," Ramsey cut in, "with Marcia dead, her husband would get her money or a big chunk of it. Then Carr could pay you off."

"You're talking nonsense," Stark said harshly. "Hand me that bag."

"No," Ramsey said. "I think I'll go to the police with it, and take my chances."

Stark hesitated, tapping a finger against his lips. He glanced again at Jefferson Carr. The lawyer's intent gaze was still on the tips of his shoes. A kind of sly smile touched Stark's lips. Still watching Carr, he spoke to Ramsey. "All right. Go to the police. It's your neck."

Carr's head shot up. "Damn it, Phil!" he blurted, "you can't let him do that! I agreed to go along with this, and you promised me he wouldn't go to the police. You—you promised there wouldn't be any trouble. You said you had him sewed up . . ."

Stark shot Jefferson Carr a quick warning glance. The lawyer's gaze wavered and once more he stared at his shoes. He sighed and said brokenly, "Phil, I just want to try and forget. I came here as a favor to you, but I—I can't stand any more." His voice quavered. "I want that man out of here. Get it over with, this—this business you say you have with him."

"In a moment, Jeff," Stark said softly.

Ramsey watched the two of them and suddenly he felt cold. And yet he was sweating. Something had seemed to blink in his memory. A tiny obscure thing, and he tried to remember. Then, frowning, he took from his coat pocket the typed message the clerk at the Gulf Hotel had given him. He stared at it, feeling like a man descending steps into black darkness and not knowing when the steps would end.

Mr. Ramsey, Room 220. 4:40 P.M. Call TEX 4999.

The little black words and the little black numbers jumped up at him, and again he thought of what the girl on the hotel switchboard had replied when he'd asked if it had been a man or a woman who had called and left the message. *It was a woman. She had a very nice voice . . .*

In the space of a second he thought of all the persons

141

he'd encountered since his arrival in the city the afternoon before. First, there had been the desk clerk at the hotel, a man. Then he'd gone to see Jefferson Carr about changing the partnership agreement. There was the Greek at the waterfront restaurant, followed by the blonde check room girl at the Jungle Tavern. Then Sara Colvin, Blake Bowen, several bartenders and taxi drivers, Phil Stark, and Victor, Stark's fat lieutenant. And he mustn't forget Sonny and Rafael. Who else, who else? What woman, except Sara and Marcia, had known that he was in town? Who was the woman who had called the Gulf Hotel? His mind raced, and once more he stared at the typed message. *Mr. Ramsey, Room 220. 4:40 P.M., 4:40 P.M. 4:40 P.M. . . .*

Ramsey sighed. Suddenly he knew. It could have been only one woman who had trapped him. It wasn't Marcia, because Marcia had been trapped, too, and she was dead. And that left only one. Carefully he folded the paper and replaced it in his pocket. He might need it as evidence, he thought bleakly, before he was finished with this. He knew who had killed Marcia, and the knowledge left him a little sick. He knew beyond doubt who had planned the trap, and lured him to Marcia's house. It had been a woman who had called the Gulf Hotel asking him to call Marcia. He had her message in his pocket. The cold type said *4:40 P.M.* That was the time she had called. A woman, with a very nice voice . . .

Phil Stark said, "Come, come, Ramsey. Let's have a look inside that bag."

Ramsey spoke to Jefferson Carr. "So you had your secretary call the hotel?"

Carr ignored him and spoke to Stark in an imploring, congested voice. "Phil, I won't have it, I tell you! I demand that you get rid of this—this person immediately." He repeated the word, shrilly, his eyes wild. "Immediately."

A quick bright flicker of interest gleamed in Phil Stark's eyes. He glanced from Ramsey to Carr, and he said soothingly, "Please try and control yourself, Jeff. I respect your feelings, and I know how grieved you must be. He will be leaving soon, I promise you."

"I want my answer first," Ramsey said, watching the lawyer.

Stark inclined his head courteously. "And you shall have an answer. It's an odd question. I admit that I'm curious as to why you asked it." He paused, smiling faintly, gazing at Jefferson Carr. Then he spoke to Ramsey. "Jeff has a secretary, of course. Her name is . . ." He snapped his fingers and looked at the ceiling.

"Whitney," Ramsey said, remembering. "Miss Whitney." He remembered everything now, all of it. The long-nosed, prim-mouthed secretary, aware that he'd been alone with Marcia that first day behind Jefferson Carr's closed office door, that he had left with Marcia, the betrothed of her employer. And she had recognized him when he had returned and had no doubt told her boss that "that man" was waiting to see him.

"Thank you," Stark said politely. "Miss Whitney, a loyal employee, Jeff has told me. Why did you ask Jeff if she had called your hotel?"

Before Ramsey could reply, Jefferson Carr said something, a blurted smudge of words, and he struggled forward from the chair, his hands gripping the arms. He started to rise, but Stark stopped him with a lifted hand. "Please," he said curtly. "There is no reason for you to get upset." He cocked his head on one side, regarded the lawyer quizzically, and added in a soft voice, "Is there, Jeff?"

Slowly Carr sank back into the chair. His eyes seemed glazed and there was sweat on his face. He stared at Ramsey and Stark, his thin lips twitching. Then he swallowed convulsively, tugged at his shirt collar with trembling fingers. "Phil, damn you . . ."

Stark ignored him and looked at Ramsey with an expression of pleasant inquiry. But Ramsey was watching Carr. Whatever Marcia had been, he thought, or had not been, she had not deserved to die the way she had. He shifted his weight and took a step toward the lawyer. The leather handle of the bag was wet with his sweat. Behind him Victor said warningly, "Take it easy," but he paid no attention.

Stark stepped between Ramsey and Carr. "Answer me," he said softly to Ramsey. "Why did you ask that question?"

Ramsey said bluntly, "Because Carr killed his wife."

For the next few seconds the only sound in the office was a kind of whimper that came from Jefferson Carr. Then Stark said to Ramsey, "Oh, come now—you don't really mean that?"

Ramsey took a deep breath. He spoke to Jefferson Carr, trying to control his voice. "Maybe I'm no good, but I don't murder people. Listen—after I left your office yesterday afternoon, you had an idea; you're in debt to Stark, here, and Marcia was going to divorce you. You didn't want to lose her—and the Stockton money. So you had your secretary call my hotel and leave a message for me to call Marcia. You figured that if I talked to her and she encouraged me, I would try and see her again. Then you told Marcia that you were going to Austin. But you didn't go. You sneaked home, watched the house, maybe even hid inside, and waited for developments. When Stark arrived, you were hiding in the house. You heard Marcia tell him that she would not pay your gambling debt. After Stark left, you waited some more, hoping that Marcia and I had taken the bait. We had. Your little trap worked. I showed up. You heard what we said to each other—about you, about the divorce. That was the right moment, while I was still with her. You shot her from the adjoining room."

Ramsey paused. His throat was dry and he swallowed. He couldn't see Victor, but Stark was watching him intently. Jefferson Carr was staring at him with haunted eyes. His mouth worked and he started to speak, but Stark silenced him with a quick impatient movement of his hand. Stark spoke softly to Ramsey. "Go on."

"That's about all," Ramsey said. "He shot her, knocked me out, planted the gun in my hand, left the house and telephoned the police, probably from a pay booth. He expected them to nab me red-handed. But Victor got me away before the cops arrived. Then, when I wasn't arrested, Carr knew that something had gone wrong, that I was still running around loose. So he called the police again, gave them my name and description, told them where I was staying. He—"

"I was in Austin!" Jefferson Carr was on his feet, trembling. "It's a damned lie, Phil! He killed my wife and now he's—"

"Stop it," Stark snapped. "You are not on trial here, Jeff."

Carr sat down again, on the edge of the chair. He glared at Ramsey. "You dirty—"

"Now, now," Stark said soothingly, smiling at the law-

144

yer. "You were in Austin, of course. You were there at the time your wife was killed. You can prove that, can't you, Jeff?"

"Certainly," Carr snapped.

Stark nodded agreeably. "Of course you can. By your hotel registration, perhaps? Or by some person who was with you in Austin last night?"

"I—I—," Carr stuttered.

"He wasn't in Austin," Ramsey said to Stark. "He never left town. He tried to rig me for a frame, so that I'd be nabbed for his wife's murder." He gave Stark a crooked smile. "At first, I thought it was you, to force me to go through with the Blake Bowen-Sara Colvin thing. I even thought that maybe you had killed her or that Victor had."

Stark shook his head reproachfully. "You thought that? No wonder you were so bitter." He sighed. "But there are holes in your story. For example, how did you know that Jeff had faked a telephone message to your hotel asking you to call his wife. You were just guessing?"

"No," Ramsey said. "It had to be Carr. The switchboard girl at the hotel told me that it was a woman who called—that threw me off. But the call came in at forty minutes past four in the afternoon, and at that time Carr and his secretary were the only persons who knew I was in town. After I registered at the hotel, I went straight to Carr's office. That was at four o'clock. I didn't return to the hotel and get the message until late last night. When I called Marcia, she said she hadn't phoned. I didn't believe her, but I wondered how she knew I'd returned from Mexico. Carr, with the help of his secretary, set up the whole thing."

Stark nodded thoughtfully. "It sounds reasonable, but I imagine Jeff will have something to say about it. We could ask Miss Whitney, too." He turned to the lawyer and smiled benignly. "Well, Jeff?"

Carr's pale eyes bulged behind the rimless glasses. "It's a lie," he blurted. "All of it. Surely, Phil, you don't believe . . . ?"

Stark lifted his tailored shoulders. "All you have to do is to prove that you were in Austin at the time of the shooting."

Carr stared at him dumbly, his mouth working.

Stark frowned and said impatiently, "You can prove it, can't you?"

"I—I don't have to prove it," Carr said thickly. "You—you told me you had enough evidence against Ramsey to convict him."

"I see," Ramsey said bitterly. "Working together, you two."

"No, no," Stark said quickly. "My business with Jeff has nothing to do with you. Because of my promise to you, I was obliged to tell Jeff of our—ah—arrangement, and to ask him to cooperate. Due to circumstances involving Jeff's indebtedness to me, he kindly agreed to refrain from turning you over to the police. But you must understand that I sincerely believed you guilty of the murder of Mrs. Carr. The evidence seemed indisputable. Now, however, in view of your statements—and Jeff's strange attitude—I must confess that a slight doubt has entered my mind." He peered at the lawyer with intense interest.

"Phil . . ." Carr's breathing was labored. "Damn it, what're you trying to pull?"

"Pull?" Stark's voice was surprised. "Why, nothing, Jeff." He gazed at the ceiling and said musingly. "Let's see—since your wife is dead, you are worth, roughly, ten million dollars." He lowered his gaze to the lawyer. "And I have your note for twenty thousand dollars. Is that correct?"

Carr lowered his head, his fingers digging into the arms of the chair. He appeared to be a man in deep thought, and seemed not to have heard Stark's question.

Stark prodded him gently. "Jeff? Twenty thousand?"

"Yes." The lawyer's one word was barely audible.

Stark sighed and said sadly, "Forgive me, Jeff. I now find that an error was made. The correct sum due me is—five hundred thousand dollars. Do you agree?"

Jefferson Carr looked up and his face seemed to shrivel. He stared at Stark slack-jawed and his eyes held a mad look. Then he sank back into the chair and covered his face with his hands. Something like a sob escaped him.

"Isn't it?" Stark insisted softly. "Isn't that the correct sum?"

There was a brief silence. Ramsey stood still, fascinated by the little cat and mouse drama. For the moment he forgot his own troubles as he watched Stark turn the screw on Carr, the screw of blackmail.

The lawyer spoke one choked, muffled word. "Yes."

Phil Stark sighed and drew himself erect. There was an exalted look of triumph, of power, in his eyes. Then he leaned toward Carr, and he seemed to have forgotten that Ramsey and Victor were in the office. Trembling a little in his excitement, he purred to Carr. "I am so sorry, Jeff. Again I seem to have made an error in—ah—calculation. I believe the final, correct sum is . . . one million dollars. Agreed?"

Carr didn't speak or remove his hands from his face. From his position by the door Victor coughed faintly and shuffled his feet.

Ramsey said to Stark, "You're over-playing your hand."

Stark ignored him, seemed not to have heard him. "Come come, Jeff," he said impatiently. "Speak up. One million dollars? It's really a small sum—comparatively. Do I have your word?"

Carr moved. He writhed in the chair as if he were enduring physical torture. And again the one word came out. "Yes."

Phil Stark straightened and turned slowly. There was sweat on his temples and his eyes held a strange wild light. From his coat pocket he took a silver case, extracted a cigarette with trembling fingers, flicked flame from a silver lighter and inhaled deeply. He stared at Ramsey almost vacantly, and smoke swirled around his head.

"You got to be a millionaire fast," Ramsey said, "but that's between you and Carr." He lifted the brown leather bag. "I don't suppose you care to bother with this small sum now?"

Stark blinked, like a man awakening. "What?"

Ramsey tapped the bag with a forefinger.

"Oh," Stark said carelessly. "Put it on the desk, please."

Ramsey said, "I get my cut—and the letter and the gun?"

"Of course. That was our arrangement."

Ramsey placed the bag on the desk. Stark opened it and gazed down at the mass of bills. His smooth white hands caressed the bundles while his lips moved in a silent tentative counting. Then he closed the bag and looked across the office at Victor, smiling thinly. He winked at Victor,

147

and then said to Ramsey, "Nice work. I'll give you a break."

"Break?" Ramsey uttered the word stupidly. He heard Victor moving behind him, and something seemed to coil in his stomach.

"Yes," Stark said pleasantly. "You deserve it. I'll wait thirty full minutes before I turn your letter and the gun over to the police. That will give you a nice little start for the Border or wherever you wish to go. You still should have most of the hundred dollars I gave you."

Ramsey didn't move or speak.

"Oh, come now," Stark said impatiently. "Surely you can understand that now I have no choice? That I must protect my friend there?" He nodded at Jefferson Carr who sat slumped like a dead man.

Ramsey heard Victor cough again. He started to speak, but Stark cut him off.

"Goodbye, sucker," Stark said.

CHAPTER 20

RAMSEY FELT SICK. He should have expected it, he told himself bitterly, when Stark had begun to suspect the truth —that Jefferson Carr had killed his wife. It was a million dollar shake-down, and he was the goat. The gun with his fingerprints on it, and his letter from Marcia, would be the clubs that Phil Stark would hold over Carr's head forever —and his head, too. Stark knew the power he held, and Jefferson Carr, in his fear of exposure, knew it, too. Stark would never give the gun and the letter to the police, because they were too valuable to him. And Victor had known all along that Stark would double-cross him, even if Jefferson Carr had not come on the scene. That was why Victor had taken the gun from him before they entered Stark's office. He, Rackwell Ramsey, was just a babe in the deep dark woods.

He thought of Marcia, a girl with too much beauty and too much money and too much time on her hands. He

148

thought of her lying still and cold in a flower-banked casket in the flossiest funeral parlor in town, with her lovely face expertly puttied, painted and powdered to hide the ugly hole where the bullet had entered. If it hadn't been for him, Marcia might still be alive. He thought of Sara Colvin, innocently loyal to Blake Bowen. Maybe Sara was dead, too, killed when he had shot at a black Cadillac and caused it to roll over in a ditch. And behind it all was the mahogany, the damned mahogany, and Nevil Simpson. He cursed Simpson, knowing that Simpson was not to blame. There was only himself to blame . . .

Phil Stark said crisply, "Get him out of here, Victor." He turned away from Ramsey, dismissing him, picked up the brown bag and moved toward the safe in the wall behind the desk.

Ramsey lunged for him. It was all that was left for him to do. Victor was behind him, but he didn't care. Stark turned a startled face as Ramsey's fist hit the side of his head. Stark swayed and Ramsey struck again, feeling a savage surge of satisfaction as his knuckles crunched against the gambler's jaw. He lashed out with both fists then, and Stark rolled against the wall, his mouth bloody. He had dropped the bag, and his hands went to his face in a protective gesture. Ramsey stepped close and hammered him viciously, blindly.

"Victor!" Stark screamed. "Victor!"

A warning signal of caution hit Ramsey's brain. He whirled to face Victor, saw that the fat man was still standing by the door. His eyes were frightened and his fat cheeks quivered. He wasn't looking at Ramsey, but beyond him, at Jefferson Carr. Ramsey turned. The lawyer was out of the chair, half crouching. His eyes were wild and his teeth were bared in a snarl. Ramsey moved for him, muttering deep in his throat, like an animal. With a terrified rodent squeak Carr scurried around the wall. Ramsey stalked him. Carr hit a corner, crouched again, his breath a hissing sound. His right hand fumbled inside his coat and snaked out holding a stubby blue-steel revolver. For an instant the muzzle wavered insanely, and then it bore on Ramsey's stomach. Ramsey stopped. Even in his rage he knew what was coming, and he felt a last wild and final despair.

Jefferson Carr laughed crazily, shrilly, and steadied the gun with both hands. Then the laugh subsided and he spoke

149

quite calmly. "Give my regards to Marcia," he said. "Tell her I'm sorry." His left hand steadied the gun's barrel, while the forefinger of his right hand crooked over the trigger.

Ramsey stood poised, suspended between the living and the dead, and he knew that whatever he did now would be futile and far too late. In the last fleeting time left to him he thought of Sara Colvin. And he jumped for Carr.

A single shot rocked the walls. Ramsey stopped and stood trembling, wondering where the bullet had struck him. But he was still on his feet, he thought with an odd detachment. Why was that? Carr couldn't have missed him at point-blank range. He stared at the lawyer. Something was wrong with him. His mouth hung open and all expression was fading from his eyes. The stubby blue gun thudded to the carpet, and Carr slid slowly down the wall until he settled on the floor in an awkward cross-legged position. In the fabric of his white shirt, just beneath the stiff collar, there was a black hole and a slowly spreading red wetness. He stirred feebly, and his breathing was a loud rasping in the sudden quiet.

As Ramsey stared dumbly, a gentle voice behind him said, "Take it easy, son." He turned slowly. Victor still stood by the door. In his hand was the .38 revolver he'd taken from Ramsey. It was now pointed at Phil Stark, who stood frozen against the wall by the safe. A tiny spiral of blue smoke curled from the gun's muzzle. Without taking his gaze from Stark, Victor said to Ramsey, "I aimed for Carr's arm, but I guess I need practice."

"Victor," Stark said from between clenched teeth, "Damn you—" He sprang for the desk and the pearl-handled gun which lay there. But Victor was faster. He stepped forward quickly, clipped Stark's extended wrist with the barrel of the .38. Stark gasped in pain and stumbled backward, holding his wrist. Victor took the gun from the desk and dropped it into a coat pocket.

Suddenly Ramsey's legs went weak. He stumbled to a chair. "Thanks, Victor," he said, and took a deep breath.

Phil Stark stood rigid holding his wrist. In contrast to the blood on his mouth and chin his face was the color of dirty snow. His eyes were blazing. From the corner where Jefferson Carr huddled there came a liquid gurgling sound. Victor glanced at Ramsey and said uneasily, "He's hit, real bad. I—I didn't mean to shoot him there. I aimed for his arm."

"You said that," Ramsey told him. "Forget it."

"He was fixing to kill you," Victor said. "Sure as hell. I just couldn't stand there and let—"

"Yes," Ramsey broke in. "It's all right, Victor. For a second there, I thought I was—never mind what I thought." He jerked his head at Stark. "You work for him. Why did you do it?"

Victor looked embarrassed. "Well, I—I had to." He coughed, avoiding Stark's outraged eyes. "I got a strong stomach, but that deal Phil tried to hand you—I couldn't take it. I told you that Phil was a square shooter and that he'd keep his word to you, and I had to do what I did. You see? You kept your end of the bargain, and I'm mighty glad you didn't kill that woman. The way I see it, you got some money coming and a letter." He gazed soberly at Stark. "How about it, Phil?"

Stark began to speak in a vicious intense voice. "You dirty, filthy, double-crossing—"

"Now, now," Victor said sharply. "None of that. There'll be no talk of double-cross—not after what you tried to do to him." He jerked his head at Ramsey. "I'm sorry, Phil. I liked my job here, but you sure disappointed me, and I'm quitting—as soon as you settle up with Ramsey."

"You stupid fool." Stark spat the words.

"Sticks and stones can break my bones," Victor said cheerfully, and waggled the gun at Stark. "Open that safe, Phil."

Stark glared a moment, hate in his eyes and a bitter frustration and something else, maybe fear. Then he turned and moved to the safe. Victor winked at Ramsey, solemnly. Stark opened the safe door and then turned to face them. As he dabbed at his bloody mouth with a handkerchief, he spoke to Ramsey in a carefully controlled voice. "Let's be sensible. I'm willing to forget what's happened and cut you in on Bowen's money. We're in the clear on that. The police won't need to know, and Bowen won't dare squawk." He looked at Victor and said grimly. "I'll cut you in, too. It'll just be between the three of us."

Victor looked at Ramsey. "Did you hear that? He's interested in small change again." He nodded at the form of

151

Jefferson Carr and said in a worried voice, "We'd better get him to a doctor or the hospital."

"A three-way split," Stark said desperately. "A hundred thousand dollars, at least, split three ways. What do you say?"

For an instant Ramsey was tempted. He had gone through a lot to get that money. Why not? Then he rejected the thought. "Just give me the gun and the letter," he said shortly.

Victor hesitated, indecision in his eyes. Then he sighed and said to Stark, "No soap, Phil. I guess both of us just got religion. All I want from you is my last pay check." He moved past Stark to the safe, took out the handkerchief-wrapped gun and Marcia's letter and handed them to Ramsey.

Ramsey stood up stiffly, pocketed the gun and letter. "Thanks, Victor. What now?"

The fat man gazed down at Jefferson Carr. "I'm sorry about him," he said soberly. Carr's eyes were closed, and they could hear his rasping breathing. As he breathed, small pink bubbles billowed from his lips. "We better call an ambulance," the fat man said.

"I'm afraid it's too late," Ramsey said grimly. He moved to the phone on the desk, ignoring Phil Stark. When Stark heard him say, "Police," he made a sudden move, but Victor stopped him by leveling the gun. Ramsey spoke briefly to a quiet-voiced desk sergeant and hung up. He said to Victor, "The cops are coming with an ambulance." He picked up the leather memorandum book from the desk, took one of the pens from the marble holder and crossed to Jefferson Carr. The lawyer stirred as Ramsey knelt beside him, but his eyes remained closed. Ramsey opened the book to a blank page, supported it on one knee and wrote: *I killed my wife, Marcia.* Then he touched Carr's shoulder and said gently, "Can you hear me?"

Carr opened his eyes slowly. There was fear in them and the cloudiness of death. Ramsey spoke close to his ear. "You killed Marcia?"

For a moment the only sound in the office was Carr's breathing. Then his lips moved and Ramsey heard the gasping whisper. "Yes . . . I—I am sorry for . . . for everything . . ." His lips kept moving, but there was no sound but the ragged breathing. Maybe he's praying, Ram-

152

sey thought, as I prayed a while ago. Carefully he placed the pen in Carr's right hand and held the pad. "Sign," he said gently.

Carr's hand moved slowly, made a scrawling signature. *J. W. Carr.* Then the pen slipped from his fingers and his eyes closed. He coughed. Blood bubbled in the hole in his throat. Ramsey tore the sheet from the pad and stood up. Victor and Stark were watching him silently. Ramsey moved to the door.

Victor's fat face puckered, like the face of a small boy about to cry, "I—I never shot a man before. I didn't mean to . . ."

"You couldn't help it," Ramsey said in a tired voice. He opened the door. "Anybody outside?" From the corner of his eye he saw Phil Stark leaning against the wall, his head down, holding the handkerchief to his mouth.

Victor shook his head. "Not yet. We don't open until five o'clock."

"We?" Ramsey asked softly.

For an instant Victor's eyes were bewildered. Then he said, "Not we, but he." He jerked his head at Stark. "Him. He don't open until five o'clock."

Ramsey nodded. "Stick around and tell the cops I'll be back."

"All right," Victor said gravely. "Uh—what about that satchel full of money?"

"Do you want it, Victor?"

"Not me. Not that money."

"Me, neither. The police can worry about it." Ramsey smiled grimly, thinking that Sara had wanted to take the money to the police in the first place.

Phil Stark spoke suddenly and harshly. "Fools, both of you. There's still time—"

"Shut up." Victor motioned with the gun, eyed Stark a moment, and then said to Ramsey. "Take the Dodge." He reached into a pocket and tossed a ring of keys. "I'll handle things here."

Ramsey caught the keys, and as he went out Victor called after him, "I hope you find her all safe and sound."

"Thanks." Ramsey felt a sudden tightness in his throat.

153

THE DAMP AIR blowing through the bullet hole in the windshield of the Dodge felt good on his face. He rounded the long curve beyond the Starlight Club and saw the black Cadillac lying on its side in the mud beyond the ditch. A state police car was parked nearby and the crew of a wreck car was working around the Cadillac. A trooper stood by the side of the road waving curious motorists on. Ramsey pulled off the road and stopped.

"Hey," the trooper called to him. "You can't stop there."

Ramsey sat quietly, his hands on the wheel.

The trooper crossed the road, waving an arm. "Get going."

When he stood by the Dodge, Ramsey said, "Anybody hurt?"

"I told you to move on."

Ramsey nodded at the wreck. "Was there a woman in the car?"

"No. Just two men."

Ramsey breathed a deep sigh. "What about them?"

"Smashed up pretty bad. Funny thing—one of 'em had a slug in his shoulder. They're in the hospital."

"That's good." Ramsey laughed a little crazily.

The trooper was a young man with a bony sun-burned face. He squinted at Ramsey suspiciously. "You been drinking, bud?"

"No."

"Lemme see your license."

Ramsey handed over his wallet.

The trooper's lips moved silently as he read. Ramsey waited.

"Ramsey, huh?" the trooper said. "Rackwell Ramsey. Hey—!" He stepped back quickly, lifted a heavy revolver from a holster. "Get out on the road, bud. Fast."

Ramsey got out.

Cars were stopping all along the road behind the Dodge.

A second trooper moved up beside the first one. "What's up, George?"

The first trooper said, "This is that Ramsey guy—wanted for murder."

"That's right," Ramsey said.

They both looked at him. "Jesus," the second trooper said.

The patrol car stopped at the entrance to the airport office. Ramsey sat in the front seat, his wrists handcuffed together. The trooper who had been driving got out and entered the building. Another trooper sat in the rear, a revolver on his knee.

In a few minutes the first trooper came out. Sara Colvin was with him. She saw Ramsey and came up to the car and gazed in at him. The trooper said, "There she is, bud. Five-two, a hundred and five, maybe a little less, blue suit, blue hat."

"Hello, Sara," Ramsey said.

"Rack, I—I was so worried. I bought the tickets, but you and that man were gone, and I waited . . ." She saw the handcuffs then and her eyes got big.

"It's all right," he said. "Everything's all right."

They held Ramsey until early evening. After the questions, they let him alone. At seven o'clock he was taken from his cell to a small bare office. A serious young lieutenant with a crew cut sat across a desk from him and said pleasantly, "You're in the clear now, Ramsey. Thanks for your help."

"You're welcome," Ramsey said and waited.

The lieutenant lit a cigarette, shoved the pack toward Ramsey, and grinned at him. "Don't you want to know what happened?"

Ramsey took a cigarette. The lieutenant held a lighter for him. "I'm a little curious," Ramsey said, smiling faintly.

The lieutenant said, "On the information you gave us, city police and federal agents raided the Jungle Tavern. They found a big cache of narcotics—heroin mostly—from across the Border. Blake Bowen is under arrest, along with a couple of men who worked for him."

"Sonny and Rafael," Ramsey said. "They're in the hospital."

The lieutenant nodded. "Under police guard."

"What about Phil Stark?"

The lieutenant shrugged. "He's a slippery character. We arrested him on general principles, but his lawyer bailed him out. We closed his club."

"And Jefferson Carr?" Ramsey asked bleakly.

"Dead," the lieutenant said soberly. "Died in the ambulance on the way to the hospital." He paused, and then said quietly, "You wouldn't have needed that confession you had him sign. Just before he died he said he killed his wife."

"Marcia," Ramsey said, more to himself than to the man across the desk.

"I believe that was her name," the lieutenant said. "By the way, here's a cablegram for you." He opened a desk drawer, took out a yellow envelope and tossed it to Ramsey. "The hotel sent it over."

Frowning, Ramsey opened the envelope, took out the sheet, and saw that it was from Nevil Simpson in Tampico. *MAHOGANY DEAL ALL SET. FOUND BACKERS WITH PLENTY OF MONEY. ANGELINE JOINING ME HERE. WANT YOU FOR BEST MAN. CABLE IF YOU NEED MONEY. WE'RE ROLLING IN IT, PARTNER . . .*

Ramsey's hand trembled a little as he folded the paper. "May I go now?" he asked the lieutenant.

"Of course. If you leave town, give us a forwarding address. You and Miss Colvin will be subpoenaed as witnesses when Bowen's trial comes up, and Mr. Herzog, too."

"Mr. Herzog?" Ramsey's voice was puzzled.

"Yes. He worked for Stark. Victor Herzog."

"Oh," Ramsey said. It was the first time he'd heard Victor's last name.

"The trial won't be for a while yet," the lieutenant said. "As I told you, if you leave here, let me know. I can fix it with the Treasury men."

"Thanks." Ramsey stood up.

"Thank you." They shook hands and Ramsey went out.

Victor and Sara Colvin were waiting for him. Victor shook Ramsey's hand gravely and said, "I got my job back at the post office. Start Monday."

"Good for you." Ramsey was watching Sara.

Victor lifted a hand. "Well, so long, folks. Think I'll take a long walk—gotta get back in shape to carry the mail." He laughed, waved his pipe. "See you around." He went out.

Sara smiled up at Ramsey. "Wyoming?"

He shook his head. "Tampico, in Mexico. Do you mind?"

"Anywhere—with you." She touched his cheek.

Ramsey sighed deeply. It seemed to him that he had been on a long dark journey, a Judas journey. But it was over now, and maybe some day he would forget it.

THE END

. . . .

"The time will come, and soon I hope, when Brotherhood Week will be a reminder, not of the presence of discrimination in our midst, but of its eradication." **— BERNARD BARUCH**

. . . .